DREW GOLDEN

Side Hustle

A Wynn Cabot Mystery

LEVEL
BEST BOOKS

First published by Level Best Books 2020

Author Photo Credit: Ken Drew for kdrewphotoarts.com

First edition

ISBN: 978-1-953789-22-8

Cover art by Level Best Designs

This book was professionally typeset on Reedsy.
Find out more at reedsy.com

Prologue

Jerusalem's outdoor cafes often feature lush trees to shade their patrons from the eastern Mediterranean sun. The sun had set after eight o'clock on this June night; by ten the pistachio trees at the Elah Café in the Jewish Quarter only added to the darkness.

Light from the fixtures on the café building barely reached to the far tables, so The Seller and his two comrades headed there. The Seller sat at one table and the other men chose a table nearby.

The Seller looked around. Quiet, save for a table of what looked like Europeans—five men and one woman dressed in waiters' shirts and aprons, all of them boisterous—sitting close to the serving station. He thought that might be good; their raucous laughter and rowdy jokes would cover any noise from what he came here to do.

He sat for a quarter of an hour, and during that time only one waiter broke from the group at the serving station to approach them. The Seller pulled a wad of bills from his pocket, stripped one off the outside and tossed it to the waiter with instructions to leave him, and the other men, alone. Scratching his head, the waiter took the bill and left the men in the dark.

Five more minutes passed, and another five. At 10:30, a stocky middle-aged American pressed his way through the tables. The blackness of the deep shade slowed him down, but he wasn't worried about thieves. He wore his travel blazer, with his wallet, passport and cash in an inside, zippered, RFID-blocking pocket.

Paying no attention to couples, families, or noisy Europeans at other tables, he headed for The Seller and stood at his table, saying nothing until The

1

Seller spoke in English.

"How can I help you?"

"You're the one who wanted to meet here."

"You don't look smart enough to be the man I'm waiting for."

The American stiffened. "I don't usually do business this way."

Shrugging, The Seller said, "There has been a development."

"You don't have it?"

"Oh, I have it," The Seller said, and from his lap placed a foot-long, rectangular package on the table.

The American reached for the package, but The Seller kept one hand on top of it and waved the palm of his other. "The price has gone up."

"How much?"

"Another ten thousand."

"I already wired you the original price." The American fought to keep his voice low and even.

"There is a competing bid."

"I'd need more time."

The Seller leaned back, his face receding into a shadow. "I am not an unfair man. You are here and ready to deal, yes? You must have some money on you for your trip, no? Give me all the money you have, and we can reach an agreement."

"But without money, I can't—"

"Jerusalem is not the far end of civilization. There are ATMs everywhere." The Seller waved his arm and then pointed a finger west. "Just don't use the one at the Joppa Gate. It's a scam."

Beads of sweat broke out on The American's upper lip. *This whole business was a scam,* he thought. But he'd come this far and wasn't going to back down now. "All right." He opened his blazer and reached his right hand in, unzipping the inner pocket.

The Seller's men saw The American reach into his jacket instead of moving his hand to his hip pocket. They jumped to their feet, shouting. One drew a gun.

Befuddled, The American withdrew a bundle from his jacket pocket. The

Seller's gunman fired.

In the darkness, the bullet went wide, but the noise of the shot echoed off nearby buildings, followed by screams, avalanches of broken dishes from overturned tables and the crash of toppled chairs as patrons ran from the cafe.

In the chaos, the Europeans turned, drawing their own guns.

One, closest to The American, raised his pistol and shouted, "Hey!"

The Seller's man aimed again, shifted his aim toward the shout, and pulled the trigger, scoring a solid hit.

Taking advantage of the distraction, The American seized the package on the table and fled.

The Europeans returned fire on The Seller's man before three of the five swarmed The Seller and his one surviving comrade. Two of them stayed behind.

The woman knelt by the injured agent, pressing her hand to the wound in his side where a bullet had left a deep gash and a shattered rib. "It would be inconvenient if you were to die in Israel," she said. "You must die at home."

Nodding between gasps, FBI Special Agent André Bishop looked up at her, and over her shoulder to the stars. He thought for a moment how beautiful they were. In the dim light, he noticed the woman was bleeding from a cut near her hairline…

And then everything went black.

Chapter One

A savage thunderstorm gathered after midnight directly over the U.S. Capitol dome and unleashed its fury on the surrounding neighborhood; hail beat leaves off the trees and ripped canvas bar umbrellas before moving on, leaving Washington, D.C. to its usual mid-June torpor.

Mark Bowles would say later that the thunderstorm, brief as it had been and though he had slept through it thanks to the whirr of a CPAP machine, signified a turning point in his life, indeed the lives of everyone around him—everything occurring either before or after a storm he never knew.

Streams of rainwater collected in pits and grooves of shell-shaped Nova Bank, where Bowles worked, and, wind-driven, water flooded into cracks in the sun-crazed surface of the gracefully curved roof. By early morning leaks had spread over the interior ceiling of the bank's lobby; rivulets finding a natural path down arms of the majestic mobile that hung from the center of the ceiling and from there out to the gold and silver elements at its ends where it collected, absorbed by the metal paint until the precious pieces blistered.

The bank's signature sculpture, *Cornucopia*, a mobile commissioned in a grand gesture to the arts from the famed sculptor Lowell Chrysler, the piece used in their logo and in all of their print collateral, the very symbol of the bank's wealth, was about to spew forth a fortune of flakes of metal paint and drip expensive rust onto the marble lobby floor below.

* * *

Three hours after opening the following morning, Peter Summers, president of Nova Bank, flashed his cuffs to exactly one-quarter inch, barely noticing the remarkable thirty-eight-foot mobile that spanned the four-way arch of the bank's soaring lobby. What he saw instead appeared to be gold and silver glitter sprinkled across the lobby floor. He slacked his trouser legs, revealing a scant glimpse of monogrammed socks, and knelt to examine the spread of twinkling fragments. Only then did he look to the ceiling.

He withdrew his handkerchief from an inside breast pocket, dabbed at the flecks on the floor, and frowned.

The gold and silver leaf of exactly the colors of the disks in the mobile that floated above the lobby now lay in quarter-sized flakes over the entire expanse of marble floor.

Except. Except in the traffic patterns, where, Summers was sure, the metallic flecks had stuck to depositors' shoe soles and been tracked out to be shed on D.C. sidewalks. Streets paved in gold, indeed.

Summers rose, felt his face flush, and glanced around. No one but employees in the front just now, and those customers who might be caught at the deposit boxes or with loan officers could be escorted out the back with an explanation of some sort or another.

"James," he called across to the security guard at the front door, "close the door and put up the sign. And then secure the lobby—let no one cross this floor until we've cleaned up this...this *mess*."

Summers dusted the flakes off his handkerchief, tucked the linen square back into his jacket pocket, turned on his Italian leather wing-tips, and strode to his office. He called maintenance first, and left instructions to sweep up the...the *very costly* debris, and bring it—in a dish—to him. And then he phoned the man who'd commissioned the piece—the bank's Vice President of Public Affairs. That bastard was going to pay for this.

Chapter Two

Not far away from the bank—less than the length of a football field—where the parking lot asphalt tapered into a weedy patch of bare land, three MPD squad cars surrounded an ambulance. All four had arrived early that morning, quietly, without lights or siren, there being no hurry.

A body lay dead in a mud puddle.

Three members of the crime scene crew, in rubber boots and latex gloves, knelt by the pool, taking photos and measurements, making notes and cracking jokes. Above and around them, uniformed officers searched the area, their vests heavy, hot and itchy as they meandered between the squad cars.

Sergeant Julie "Frosty" Winters stood at the edge of the puddle, tilted her head, and squinted.

The corpse was anomalous.

Not just because it was female, although the MPD didn't get too many dead females in this part of town—the exceptions being homeless and hookers—this one didn't look like either. That was another thing that made this one an anomaly: she was dressed expensively, one of those outfits in the stark black and white ads that spread across two pages in the fashion magazines.

She lay in the rainbow-spectrum-oil-slicked water, her Tory Burch shoes still on her feet, legs splayed but none of the usual signs of rape.

No, Winters realized, the body registered off-kilter because although she lay on her stomach, she was face up—her head having been twisted a hundred and eighty degrees on her neck, the un-muddied nose and cheeks above the water level, but shoulder blades where breasts should have been.

Winters moved closer to the crime scene crew. "Who found her?"

"Security guard for one of these office buildings," one of them said.

"Did he move her?"

"No. He figured with her head like that, there was a pretty good chance she was dead. I mean, usually, you put two fingers on the neck, find a pulse. But when the neck is..."

Winters sniffed. "Got a time of death yet?"

He shook his head. "Too many factors—a wet night that heated up when the rain stopped. But in the water like this, the body temp's not a good gauge." He glanced from one crew member to the other. "Still, if she wasn't here yesterday and she is now..."

She looked up at the merciless sun, the parking garage, the nearby overpass. "Any footprints? Anything?"

"Yeah, we got footprints—about six hundred of them. Not a one we can use. God almighty, this mud's so churned up, we can barely work. It's like the entire sixth fleet got shore leave and marched through here. Geesh."

"You about done?"

He snapped a final photograph. "I guess. We're going to want to get anything we can out of the water. In the meantime, let's lift her out of there."

The three crew members, assisted by the EMTs from the ambulance, did the work, lifting the corpse rather than turning it over and getting the dry side wet. As they slid the body onto a stretcher, Winters asked for another look at the face.

She sighed.

"You know her," the duty cop said. It wasn't a question.

"Know who she is. Was." Winters inspected her shoes for mud. "One of the Arazis. I think her name's Rima."

"Oh, yeah." The cop's face registered, remembering. "Her daddy went on trial awhile back for black market deals."

"And the lovely Rima stood by his side. Not so lovely now."

"What a soap opera that was."

Winters nodded. Soap opera was a perfect description. And she'd give anything to see the script for this episode—to explain what Rima Arazi had been doing down here in this precinct on a rainy June night.

Chapter Three

Mark Bowles had spent his banking career as an advocate for the people, and while he liked that about himself, he was disappointed that it hadn't yet got him the coveted corner office. Yes, being Vice President of Public Affairs for Nova Bank meant he got good tickets to basketball games and operas, and he enjoyed those things, as did Mrs. Bowles.

But Mrs. Bowles was far more ambitious for her husband.

He had explained to her again just now, in a testy—and, on his end, whispered—phone call, why he thought he might move to a job that had been offered to him by one of the larger chain banks up on K Street, rather than stay with Nova, where there was only one chance for advancement, and that was to Peter Summers' job.

Summers wasn't going anywhere.

Bowles' phone rang again, and he looked at the readout: Summers. *Dear God*, he thought, *had Summers overheard his end of the conversation with the Missus?* He gulped and picked up the receiver.

"I have an issue that needs your attention," Summers said. "Could I ask you to meet me, as they say, in the lobby?"

Summers hung up and smiled to himself. That was a witty remark he'd just made to Bowles. He'd always considered himself humble for as high-born and intellectual as he was. His carriage and cleft-chin good-looks spoke, of course, to his breeding. His success was due to his business acumen, sense of market timing, keen people skills.

But he was, he thought, in spite of those gifts, a decent human being. After all, when he called Bowles, the poor sap never suspected the shit storm that was in store for him when Summers showed him the detritus from the mobile.

The mobile was the bank's single most valuable piece of artwork—its arms of platinum rods balanced leaf-shaped solid gold and silver disks—composed of seven elements and twenty-three impressive leaves, and over all large enough to be seen from the street. Exactly what the bank's owners, Howard and Sherryl Jacobs, had in mind. A show-stopper. A people-pleaser. Everyone who banked with Nova felt a sense of financial confidence as they entered the lobby.

Now, it seemed, the mobile wasn't what it purported to be. The leaves weren't—or weren't at first blush—solid gold and silver, but gold and silver overlay. Overlay that was now coming loose and falling to the floor like paint off a God-damned Jackson Pollock painting.

Were the Jacobses to find out that their considerable investment was a fraud, Summers feared his days in the corner office would be over. He was the one who had convinced them that the bank needed a signature piece. Oh, Bowles would have to go too, since he was the one who had commissioned the work from Chrysler, but Summers knew the Jacobses would ask for his resignation first.

He could say goodbye to his banking career in the white-shoe hub of Washington, D.C. He would be finished.

* * *

The minute Mark Bowles saw Summers standing over the maintenance man as he swept the last of the precious metal flakes off the lobby floor, he braced for the worst—which was what he got after he and Summers returned to Summers' office, Summers carrying the dish of gold and silver leaf.

Summers postured and threatened, towered and scowled. But his tantrum went sideways when he took up the dish of metal flakes and threw a fistful at Bowles while he cursed the day he'd hired him.

The bits floated serenely in the air for a moment, flickering in the light like dust motes, lending a sudden festive moment to Summers' tirade. Bowles stepped back, out of the landing pattern, and the glitter settled onto an Oriental carpet in front of Summers' desk.

Both Bowles and Summers stared at the sparkly mess on the carpet for a moment, and then Bowles spoke. "Well. That's it then. May I say, sir, that I've been offered a position at another bank and you've made my mind up for me. You have my two weeks' notice, effective now. I'll be leaving at the end of the month." He turned and walked toward the door.

"Get back here. You're not leaving this office *or* this bank."

"I am, sir. Doing both." He reached for the door knob.

"What other bank would have you?"

"I don't think I need to say I've been offered positions at several banks. I'm sure you'll find out soon enough where I've gone."

"I'll ruin you."

Bowles blew out a breath and smiled. "You won't, sir. I have that assurance in a file I keep. Mr. and Mrs. Jacobs would be interested to see what's in that file."

"You wouldn't—there's nothing I've done that...how dare you? You're leaving this...our family because..."

"Because you've lost your temper with me once too often." He snickered. "And this time you threw glitter."

By the time Bowles re-crossed the lobby to his office, James Roybal, front door security, was at his side, handing him a cardboard box. "Summers says I'm to walk you out. Get what you need out of your office and come with me." They walked the length of a carpeted hallway in silence before Roybal said, "You get fired?"

"I quit." Bowles stopped and leaned on a wall, laughing. "He threw glitter at me."

Roybal snickered. "The stuff off the floor? Wait'll he sees what's on that floor now. Roof's started to leak after the rain last night and the sculpture's rusting. Dribbling yellow water all over his nice shiny marble. He's going to lose his mind." Now Roybal laughed. "Ah, God, Bowles, you're lucky to be getting out of here." Roybal snorted back a giggle and gestured toward

Bowles's office door. "Go get your stuff. Take as long as you need. The bank's closed until further notice because…" He leaned his hands on his knees and laughed again, silently, his shoulders shaking. "…Because the roof is pissing on us."

Bowles placed photographs and mementoes in the cardboard box and sat for a moment, looking around the room, feeling as though he should do something other than simply rise and walk out of his office.

He should call his wife and tell her he'd resigned.

He should call the outfit that had offered him the latest job and take it before they hired someone else.

He should go into Summers' office, apologize, and say he would stay.

No.

No, he should not do any of that. Not from here. And he should not apologize to Summers at all. Ever.

What he did instead was step to a locked filing cabinet, unlock it, and pull out the second drawer. He felt for the small envelope taped to the right inside wall of the cabinet, near the back, pulled the envelope loose, withdrew a key, dropped it in his pocket and tossed the envelope in the wastebasket. He picked up the cardboard box full of personal effects and his briefcase, and met Roybal in the hallway.

"Need to make one stop," he said. "Safe deposit box. Got my passport and some bond stuff there."

"Marlene's on duty—she's got the other keys today."

"Fine. I'd like to say goodbye to her anyway."

They paused in front of the elevator to the secured vault.

Bowles pulled his employee badge out of his jacket pocket and held it to the prox scanner near the elevator door. As the door opened Roybal plucked the ID from his fingers. "You won't be needing this again, right?"

"Yeah, no. No, I won't, I guess."

"Sorry, Mark."

"It's okay. I understand."

They took the elevator two floors down to a small antechamber where Marlene Reese, a retired relative of the Jacobs family, sat at a small desk, reading a dog-eared romance novel. The three-ton steel vault door stood open on the far wall.

"Hey, Mark, hey James. What gives with the box? You need more safe deposit space? We've got one big one left."

Bowles set the box on Marlene's desk and held out his hand. "Not after today, Marlene, though I admire you for trying to sell me something. No, I'm leaving Nova today. For good. It's been a pleasure working with you."

She shook his hand warmly and smiled. "Mark! What? No! Howard and Sherryl will be so disappointed to see you go. A better job, I bet. Out from under Snarky Summers. Remember me if they need someone with my talents."

"Just need into my box one last time, please. 189."

Marlene took her wheel of keys and used a large one to open the metal gate inside the vault door, giving the two of them access to the safe deposit room. They crossed to number 189. Both of them inserted their keys, turned them a quarter-turn to the left, and the small metal door opened. Bowles slid his box out and took it to a table in the center of the room. He turned to Marlene and handed her his key.

"All yours after today. Thank you for being so gracious to all of us here at the bank—I know you don't enjoy being cooped up in a windowless room for hours on end." He frowned. "Say, that's a nasty cut on your forehead..."

Marlene fingered the purplish wound, the edges of the gash bandaged at the center with a butterfly patch, and shrugged. "Coming home from vacation, a piece of luggage fell out of an overhead compartment on the plane. I'd like to say, 'You should've seen the other guy,' but the other guy was a pink makeup case. I'll live." She sighed. "We'll miss you, Mark."

He chucked the older woman under the chin. "You sure it's not those Nats tickets you'll miss?"

"I'll admit I'll miss those, too. You were generous with your swag. I'll leave you to it and go flirt with James for a few minutes."

Bowles lifted the lid on his safe-deposit box and withdrew its contents: his and his wife's passports, a batch of bearer bonds and Treasury notes, and a file folder—the contents of which were worth far more than the rest of the paper combined: his insurance that neither Peter Summers nor anyone else in modern-day banking would have the ability to ruin his career—photos, emails and banking forms that were enough to bring Nova Bank to its knees.

A life in Public Affairs had been good to him, but now it was time for a bigger payday.

Chapter Four

Wynn Cabot brushed imaginary specks of lint from her skirt as she waited for the Art Crimes Program Manager, Linda Grazer ("Ma'am" to her face, "Here's the Deal Grazer" behind her back) to finish her call. Wynn couldn't imagine why she'd been summoned to Grazer's office, although a few less-than-favorable scenarios came to mind. Despite her success with the case last Thanksgiving in California wine country, she'd had a slow start with the Bureau and only minor successes—recoveries of smaller works and uncovering two solid leads—since the holidays. She hoped she wasn't here to be handed a pink slip.

As she stared at the items on the credenza behind the section chief, Grazer, all no-nonsense, abruptly ended her call.

"Sorry, Cabot, I had to take that. Okay. Here's the deal." Grazer steepled her fingers. "André Bishop's been gone a few days."

Wynn's senses went to high alert. She wasn't actually going to be canned while her supervisor was away. Was she?

"Actually," Grazer said, "he's away on assignment to assist another agency with a recovery operation."

"Can I ask where?"

"No. That info's limited to people who need to know. But here's the deal. The recovery operation exploded. Bishop was injured."

Wynn's jaw dropped. "Is he—did he—"

Grazer leaned forward. "He survived. Don't worry about Bishop. But—"

"Where is he?"

15

"Need to know."

"Can I see him?"

"No. Cabot, don't—"

"How did this happen?" Wynn fought to keep her voice from rising from Shrill setting to Tantrum.

"It's part of the job. Occupational hazard. Set that aside and listen to me."

Stunned, Wynn took three deep breaths. "Yes, ma'am."

"All right. Until Bishop returns, *if* he returns, you report to me. Understood?"

"*If* he returns?"

"Understood?" Grazer repeated.

Still gulping deep breaths, Wynn said, "Yes. ma'am."

"Great. Get back to work."

Wynn rose. The weight of the news pressed on her like water and she fought the current, pushing out of Grazer's office.

Back at her desk, she fumed. Hadn't she sworn an oath to bear faith and allegiance to the country? Did they think they couldn't trust her because she was a rookie?

She knew enough to know she was not the risk here. Bishop's assignment, whatever it was, must have been so top-secret that the number of people who knew about it could be counted on one hand.

She needed a plan.

Casually she began deliberately rifling through her desk drawers as though she was looking for something. Slamming the last drawer in mock frustration, she strode to Bishop's desk, searching for anything that might tell her where he'd gone.

One of the other agents looked up. "You lost, Cabot?"

She spoke without glancing up. "I need the contact for that Los Angeles gallery where the Parrish panels went missing. You don't have it, do you?"

He waved her off. "You and Bishop drew that one."

"Yeah." She sighed audibly. Bishop's desk was regulation-clean, computer turned off and drawers locked. She'd almost given up when she looked under his keyboard and spied a stack of scraps—business cards, slips with phone

numbers, email addresses, coffee coupons and—yes. One sticky note with
the letters and numbers:

IAD TLV 612

Sticking it to her index finger, she said absently, "Got it," and went back to
her own desk. IAD, she knew, was the airport code for Washington's Dulles
Airport. And June 12 was the day he'd left. So, it was simply a matter of...

Her fingers poised over her keyboard, she hesitated, remembering what
Grazer had said. If anyone was watching her Internet searches, she'd be
busted. She could wait, she thought, a little while anyway. She was meeting
her friend Giovanni Leo tonight, so she didn't have the entire evening to
search for Bishop.

But she didn't need an entire evening. She needed an anonymous phone
with a data plan, and she could get that at the Walmart on H Street on her
way over to Mount Vernon Square. She had a date.

She'd convinced Giovanni "Gio" Leo, the FDA investigator she'd met on
the California case last Thanksgiving, to come into D.C. for a drink instead
of making her trek out to FDA headquarters in Maryland. They sat in a
booth at The Side Hustle, a few blocks from the FBI building.

"The guy that owns this place owns the restaurant next door," she said. "But
he wanted more than a burger joint, so when the previous tenants moved
out he grabbed it. Calls it his side hustle."

"Traffic into D.C. is worse than ever, and there's never anywhere to park,"
Leo said.

She smiled. "Mm-hm, first world problems."

"Not necessarily. Traffic's bad in third world countries too, believe me."

She smiled. Leo, she had learned in the short time they'd been friends, was
an inveterate traveler. "You're probably right."

Sipping his wine, he looked at her over the rim of his glass. "You're
distracted. I come all the way across the country, drive into Washington
because you asked me to, spend thirty bucks on parking, and your mind's
somewhere else."

"I'm sorry," she said. "I was thinking how much easier life would be if
everyone who owned a valuable piece of art put a GPS locator on it. That

way, we'd always know where it was. Or maybe," she held up a palm, "artists should build in locator chips when they're creating the works."

"A LoJack for artwork. I'll tell Rembrandt next time I see him. Oh, wait. He's still dead. Isn't a lot of art valuable because the artist is dead?"

Over the months, as their familiarity had become friendship with a hint of something more, their banter included occasional zings and buzzkills. "You know what I mean."

Now he laughed with her. "I do. But if all art had GPS locators on it, you'd be minus a job. And I'd be minus a girl—" He stopped. "A good friend."

He cocked his head to one side. "So, tell me now. What's really bothering you?"

She looked into her glass. She'd never be good at poker, not with her feelings that transparent on her face. "I'm sorry. My boss, André Bishop—I think you met him last fall in California—he was...injured in the line of duty."

"Injured? Is he okay?"

"That's just it." She tried to cover the catch in her voice. "The higher-ups won't read me in. I don't know where he is, or the extent of his injuries."

"Geez, honey, anything I can do?"

"You're sweet to offer, but no. If the operation really was covert, I don't want to do anything to endanger him, or you, or me. Or our jobs."

Leo whistled low and covered her hand with his own. "You know, all you have to do is ask."

She turned her own hand up to grasp his. "Thanks. That means a lot. But I've got a couple things to check out first."

Maps were one thing Wynn did well with, despite her dyslexia. Her dyslexia probably helped. Even a brief glance at a two-dimensional surface and she could tell the spatial relationships between cities, waterways, forests, historic markers and roads. She retreated to her tiny apartment in North West Washington—one she'd rented because she was tired of living at the Residence Inn while the Bureau debated what to do with their crumbling headquarters building—and opened her laptop.

She looked up the airport code that was the destination written on the sticky note: TLV.

Tel Aviv.

Pulling up a map of the eastern Mediterranean, she studied it for several minutes before she made several conclusions:

First, if Bishop was assisting another agency in that region, it would be a friendly agency in a friendly country.

Next, other friendly countries in that area would have their own international airports—or U.S. military installations.

Third, if Bishop flew to Tel Aviv, the operation probably went down in Israel somewhere. Otherwise, he would have flown into a different airport.

She sat back. She couldn't call him directly, not yet. Not until she knew he himself would answer, not someone else, and certainly not anyone in law enforcement. She had to make sure he was awake and able to speak. How would she find that out in a country the size of New Jersey?

Hospitals.

A quick Wikipedia search brought up hospitals in Israel, and from there she had only to pick out the ones who could handle trauma. *With a history such as Israel's,* she thought, *probably a lot of facilities had found the need to handle trauma.*

She checked the clock on her screen: almost midnight, and with the seven-hour time difference, that made it early morning in Tel Aviv. Activating her phone, she made the first round of calls.

With all of them, the conversation went the same: "Hello, I'm calling to check the status of a patient, André Bishop." None of them had a patient by that name.

Pausing, she doodled on a scratch pad. She didn't know for sure if Bishop was there under a fake name, or if he really wasn't there. The only thing she could do was expand the search.

She scrutinized Wikipedia's list: pausing over Hospitals in Haifa, her eyes dropped to the next region down.

Jerusalem.

She cursed herself for not seeing it before. If there were art crimes to solve in Israel, they would be there, in the ancient city where the art, the relics, even the land is contested by people, religions and politics. She dialed the first hospital on the list, Shaare Zedek.

And was put through to the nurses' station.

Wynn found herself grabbing for a tissue and blotting her eyes as the nurse said, "Yes. He is here and quite satisfactory."

"Is it possible I could speak with him?"

"He is receiving therapy. It is difficult for him to speak."

"He can't talk?"

"The collapsed lung, you know. But he improves every day. May I suggest you call again tomorrow?"

"I'll do that," Wynn said. "Thank you for your help."

Wynn rang off, staggered to her bed, pulled relief over herself like a blanket and fell asleep as soon as she closed her eyes.

Chapter Five

The estimator from Versailles Art Transport didn't match the company's palatial name; he looked like a stand-in for ZZ Top's Billy Gibbons, with his long, scraggly beard, sunglasses and hat. He stroked the beard thoughtfully while he looked at the floor. "We'll have to put down pressboard," he said.

Roybal folded his arms. Estimates for moving artwork weren't in his wheel house, but Summers had barked out an order to deal with the mess since the managers were all busy "with real jobs," and the estimator needed an escort at all times. "Pressboard? For what?"

The Beard pointed his sunglasses to the ceiling. "To get up there," he said, "we'll need a man-lift. We've got one that's narrow enough to come through the front door. But it'll weigh several hundred pounds itself, and when we roll it over here, it could crack your lovely marble. Or leave tire marks. Or both." He stroked the beard gently. "We pride ourselves on taking care of the environment as much as we take care of your art."

Roybal sincerely hoped that was true, since the man didn't take much care with his own appearance. His nails were grimy and there was what looked like dried mustard caked into the beard along his jaw line.

"So that'll take a while," The Beard said, "and then we take down each piece, one, maybe two at a time. You figure going up there and down that many times, pack everything in pads in the truck, take up the pressboard, it'll take most of a day."

Roybal puffed out his cheeks. Summers wasn't going to love that. "When can you come get it?"

"It so happens, tomorrow's a good day. But I have to warn you, the boom lift makes a lot of noise, kind of a whiny 'scree.' Your customers aren't going to like it."

The customers aren't the only ones, Roybal thought. "Let me check with the brass and let you know."

The Beard pulled a card from the pocket of his plaid shirt and handed it over, then put two fingers to his temple in a mock salute. "You know where to find me."

Roybal's guess about Summers was correct: the boss was livid about possibly closing the bank. Roybal forced himself to remain impassive as Summers fumed and fussed, accused Roybal of incompetence and then instructed him to once again close the bank while the sculpture was dismantled and taken away. "I won't even bother to come in," he said. "You take care of it."

The following day, Roybal kept busy, letting The Beard and his co-workers in, holding the door as they brought in the pressboard and the personnel lift, watching as they photographed the mobile from every angle—"to remember how to put it back together," The Beard had said—and keeping the customers out, with suitable firmness and sufficient apologies.

At 11:45 the phone at the reception desk rang. And rang.

Roybal paused in his supervisory duties and picked it up. "Nova Bank. Roybal here."

"Who the hell are you?" a male voice demanded.

The boom lift screeched loudly as it made another ascent to the ceiling.

"Sir? Roybal. Security, sir."

"Where the hell is Summers? And what's that noise?"

"Sir, the bank is closed today, sir."

"Whose God damned idea was that?"

"Sir, may I suggest you call back—"

"This is Howard Jacobs, damn it! I got a call from a customer that you're closed and I want to know what the hell's going on!"

"Sir, the bank is closed while the sculpture is removed so the ceiling can be repaired. Sir."

"Well, damn it, get it done and get the bank open! I'm holding you responsible." The line went dead.

Roybal chuckled and hung up. He could leave now, he could announce to no one in particular that he quit and walk out the door. He had been drafting his own big plans for the future. He wasn't going to be a bank guard forever, but he wasn't going to wreck his resume by deserting his post before his next gig was a dead certainty.

* * *

By late afternoon the last of the mobile's arms had come down, along with the harness that attached the entire thing to the ceiling. As with all of the other pieces, they were placed in a felt bag, the bag wrapped in moving blankets, and the final bundle was piled on the restoration company's dolly along with tools and broken pieces of pressboard.

The Beard shoved a clipboard at Roybal. He signed to indicate the work had been done and let the crew out.

Turning back to the room, he gazed upward. The sculpture—*Cornucopia*—had been gaudy and crass and a symbol of material greed, he thought, but it was a promise, a fortune you might attain if you worked hard and climbed higher for it, money always in sight but ever out of reach.

He checked his watch. One more appointment before quitting time.

Through the front door he watched as Versailles Art Transport loaded the last of their tool bags, the sculpture, and the man-lift onto their vehicles and pulled away, just as Narville Phelps Construction Company's trucks pulled up, two flat-beds of scaffolding in tow.

Roybal opened the door once again, and the roof repairmen unloaded metal frames and duffle bags containing nail guns, hammers, and various sealants, arraying it all on padded blankets so as not to scratch the bank's marble floors. They assembled their scaffolding quickly under the site of the leak, climbed down and, with assurances that they'd be back at 9:00 a.m. and done by lunch, they left.

Roybal checked his fitness watch—quitting time. He closed and locked the front door and set the alarms. Tomorrow, Friday, would be a bank holiday in observance of the Fourth of July, which fell on Saturday. He'd need to work only as long as the roof repairmen were in the building.

His spirits lifted, as spirits will when an extra-long weekend stretches ahead as an expanse of happy territory. After closing the bank tomorrow afternoon, he'd hit the gym, and maybe find a date for the fireworks at the National Mall on Saturday night.

Wynn's follow-up efforts to reach Bishop at the hospital in Israel weren't going smoothly. Two nights ago, the nurse had suggested Wynn call again the next day; but when she dialed Bishop's cell phone, the calls kept dropping, and she'd given up out of frustration.

Today, though, she knew the call would go through, *willed* it to go through.

She heard a muffled groan and labored breathing. A voice croaked, "Bishop."

"André, it's Wynn. Don't talk unless you're alone."

"Wynn," he rasped out. "Yes. No one here. But—" He took a long but shallow breath. "You shouldn't...be calling..."

"I know. I know. But I was worried, and...telling me not to call is like waving a red cape in front of me. I just, I wanted—"

Her depth of feeling took her by surprise. Still, she passed it off. *Of course I care about him. He's my boss.*

"—I wanted to know that you're going to pull through, and that you're coming home."

He sucked in another swish of air. "Yes, on both counts. I'm—" Another breath. "I'm on the mend."

"Oh, that's great news."

"I can start home next week. But they said—" He paused for a long moment, choosing his words for brevity. "No high altitude. Short flights only. No more than an hour or two."

"I understand. Only—can you keep me advised?"

"I really shouldn't."

"Oh." The disappointment in her voice echoed through the line.

"What is this number?" he wheezed.

"Burner phone."

"I'll text you." With that, the line went dead.

She looked at her phone. No goodbye, no thanks for calling. But then, what did she expect? He could barely talk, and she wasn't supposed to have contacted him in the first place.

He'd said he'd text and keep her advised of his progress home—he was coming home. She hugged her phone to her, precious little life line, magic window to halfway around the world.

In his bed at Shaare Zedek, Bishop closed his eyes. He no longer drifted in and out of consciousness—the anesthetic from the surgery had worn off—but he needed peace and quiet, and to shut out the world for a while.

Wynn's call should have comforted him, but it did the opposite. On the surface, he was angry she'd found him; he didn't want her compromising the mission, cracking his cover—or anyone else's. He trusted her enough not to do that, but in his present condition, he felt...well...vulnerable.

If anything went wrong—anything else—he wasn't sure he could defend himself. He didn't like that feeling.

That was the other reason he was upset. In the restaurant that night, he'd made a mistake. No, that wasn't exactly true; he'd done what he thought was right, and it turned out to be an error in judgment.

An error that got him shot.

Groaning, he turned onto his right side, trying to get comfortable. It didn't work.

What if someone else had been hurt because of his error in judgment? What if someone on the law enforcement side had been killed? Would it have been worth it, to lose a life over a piece of art?

What if he himself had died that night?

What if it had been Wynn? His stomach went cold, and he shivered. But it wasn't Wynn, he thought. He didn't die, and now he had to deal with the fallout.

He shifted position again and pain sliced through the left side of his torso.

First, he had to deal with Wynn. He knew she wouldn't let up until she'd seen him and knew he was back to being his old self—bad with women, cheap

25

with a dollar, good at his job. Or at least he'd thought he was good at his job until…this.

He'd keep Wynn advised, but out of the loop. Feed her a bare minimum of progress, but at arm's length or more from the case. The botched sale here in Jerusalem had complicated things for all the parties—and agencies—concerned. It would take weeks just to debrief, compare notes, and figure out what to do next.

Well, he wouldn't be doing much else, he figured.

Job one was to put himself back together, on his feet, into shape.

He shifted once more, trying to push up into a sitting position, so he could swing his legs over the side of the bed. Lifting his upper body, however, was more than he could do without help.

Dropping back onto the pillows, he shivered again and closed his eyes.

But not to sleep. He wouldn't sleep, not well, while the pain was bad. He didn't want too many painkillers while he felt vulnerable. If he were honest, he told himself, he wouldn't sleep until he was on his way home.

Here in Jerusalem, he was a sitting duck.

But once he got home, how would he cope with Wynn?

Chapter Six

Nova Bank, nestled on a pie-shaped wedge of land to the west of a Verizon switching office on E Street Southwest, sat at one corner of one of the most surveilled sites in Washington, D.C.; the city itself one of the most surveilled in America. Howard Jacobs, owner of Nova Bank, liked it that way. He'd chosen the site for its security.

At one end of E Street sat Metro Police's First District substation, and at the other, MPD's Forensics Lab. Police cruisers passed by the bank regularly.

Across the street from the bank sat an unmarked, and unremarkable, government building whose only identifier was a guard station; its sign read "IDs checked 100%."

Next to that, on the same side of the street, an office building in which Congressman B. Crawford Dawson had, months ago, taken an office on the third floor, and marked the door PRIVATE. There was no other identifying mark to the office, nor was his name listed on the building directory downstairs. The office's only window had a clear view of Nova Bank, across the street.

Three security companies—two of which contracted internationally—also occupied several floors of the building. Job-hunting mercenaries mingled in the lobby with secretaries and messengers.

For its part, the switching station building, a bunker-like structure with arrow-slit windows, had more activity than a mere telephone installation should. Black SUVs with smoked-glass windows and license plates that bore only single or double digits came and went hourly. The neighborhood rumor mill had it that the building was a covert NSA site.

Between the routine police presence on the street, an imposing unmarked government building next to an office tower full of guerilla contractors, the Verizon bunker with its mysterious visitors, and more than a handful of closed-circuit cameras on the outdoor corners of each, not to mention a clutch of cell towers up the street, Jacobs felt Nova Bank was secure enough with what few protections he'd put in place.

Congressman B. Crawford Dawson had moved a desk, a chair, two filing cabinets and fifteen philodendron plants into the small office space. Posing as Howard Jacobs, Crawford fired the plant-care firm that tended Nova bank's various plants and hired a landscape firm to tend his philodendron as well as the flora both inside and out in front of Nova Bank.

The new company, Planties and Bloomers, was comprised of just one man—a man with a passing knowledge of horticulture, but a thorough mental index of the streets of Washington D.C.: which way they ran, where they began and when they became narrower or wider, where the alleys were and whether they were dead-ends.

Dawson looked out the office's one window, watching the smattering of foot traffic on E Street, cops and government heavies strewn with the occasional unsuspecting shlub headed for the dentist's office on the first floor of his building or secretary headed to the Capitol Café to fetch her boss's lunch.

His view of Nova Bank's dramatic arches, and its front door, were ideal from here, which made the broom-closet-sized room with the rent bill of a Manhattan penthouse worth every penny.

Narville Phelps found the office he sought and opened the door.

Congressman Dawson jumped, startled, and laid his phone face down on the desk. "Everyone likes to walk through a door marked Private, don't they, Phelps?"

"I didn't notice." Phelps looked again at the office door. "Oh. Oh yeah. What was I supposed to do, knock?"

Dawson shook his head. "You're in now. What do you want?"

Phelps jerked a thumb toward E Street, outside. "Team's over there at the bank, fixing the roof. Thought I'd let you know."

Dawson nodded. "As they should be. Why aren't you watching them?"

"Can't. Heights—I don't like them."

"I see. You're more of a feet-flat-on-the-floor kind of fella?"

"Yeah. Flooding in your kitchen and like that. None of this crawling around up high. Gets me all woozy."

"But you have a construction company, I thought."

"Yeah. And?"

"How do you handle…? Never mind." Dawson considered Phelps' size for a moment. "You work out, Phelps?"

"Every day. Haven't missed a day in years."

"What do you press?"

"On a good day I can dead-lift 350 pounds. What of it?"

"I'm always on the lookout for strong talent, Phelps. For personal jobs. Interested?"

Chapter Seven

Howard Jacobs smiled as he drove down Wisconsin Avenue toward the center of town and Nova Bank, a wide, self-satisfied grin that spread across his face, squared his shoulders and warmed his heart. The rabbi at Temple Chesed—the most prestigious synagogue in D.C.—had, in return for a gift the Jacobses recently conferred, appointed Jacobs as a Trustee.

The gift, a companion piece to the priceless 15th Century Samaritan codex he'd come by at no small personal risk, sat next to him on the passenger seat of his Mercedes SL roadster, wrapped in multiple layers of burgundy velvet and swaddled in a blue and white prayer shawl. The book itself, bound in maroon leather, had moved many times over the centuries, and he and his rabbi prayed the codex had finally found a home in Temple Chesed. For now, though, the codex resided in a safe deposit box held in the rabbi's name, in the basement vault at Jacobses bank.

After years of two-bit investment hustles and flailing around in the securities markets, he was finding his footing as a banker. And with the purchase of these items from overseas sources, he considered himself an international financier. He smiled again, liking the sound of it—Howard Jacobs, Temple Trustee, and international financier.

Anyone who saw Howard Jacobs enter Nova Bank, walk across the lobby and press the elevator button would have sworn he was an average-looking guy in his fifties, sandy haired and paunchy, with a couple loaves of French bread in a paper bag. They might have wondered why the guy was taking French bread to a bank vault, but nothing more; Jacobs was that unremarkable.

Jacobs rode down and stepped out of the elevator. At her desk, Marlene Reese looked up from her book and smiled a greeting.

"Can it, Marlene," Jacobs snarled. "I need a bigger safe deposit box."

"Of course." She retrieved the keys and began the process of opening the vault door. "How was your trip to—Cleveland, wasn't it?"

"Cincinnati. Good thing you have a computer to keep these boxes organized, since you can't keep anything else straight in your head."

She opened his small box for him, and then bent to insert the keys into a large, floor-level box. Presenting him with his new key, she said, "I'll leave you to it, Howard. Will you be keeping the small box?"

"No. Only the big one now."

"I'll update that computer record." She left him in the vault to empty his small box into the big one and add the contents of the paper bag.

When he finished, he called her and they closed the box and left the vault.

Jacobs regarded Marlene for a moment, his upper lip curling. "What the hell happened to your head? Cover that cut up, can you? It's disgusting. And call Summers. Tell him to meet me at the elevator."

"Right away, Howard."

She picked up the phone. She could have sworn that last week he'd said the conference was in Cleveland. Speaking into the receiver, she smiled at Jacobs' back as he got on the elevator.

Jacobs waited while Summers double-timed it to meet him at the elevator. Grabbing Summers' shoulder, Jacobs turned him around and steered him back toward his office.

"I need to talk to you."

Summers looked around the lobby while he ran a hand through his steel-gray hair. "Sure, Howard."

"I need you to do something for me. Again."

Summers swallowed hard. "Again?"

Jacobs looked up at the empty ceiling. "Yes, again. But first, you can start by getting the mobile put back up."

"Well, we need to make sure everything's copacetic up there. That there are no more leaks."

"Get the damned sculpture back up."

"Then the repairs need to be load-tested."

"Did you hear me?"

"We shouldn't rush things—"

"Damn it!" Jacobs pointed at Roybal. "You!"

Roybal sprang to his feet as Jacobs' voice echoed off the marble and glass. "Give me the name of the art moving company."

Roybal grabbed the Versailles business card from under a monitor and hustled around the desk. He handed the card to Jacobs, who had already pulled his phone from his jacket pocket.

"God damn shame I have to do everything myself," Jacobs said as he thumbed in the numbers and put the phone to his ear.

The last thing he heard before his meltdown was, "The number you have reached is not in service at this time…"

Ten minutes later, his collar soaked from the cold water he'd splashed on his face, Jacobs exited the men's room to find Summers waiting by the door.

"Here's your phone," Summers said. "I think the screen broke when you threw it."

Jacobs snatched the device from Summers' hand. "We're going to your office and have a little chat. You're going to do what I ask, damn it. Then you'll call the police and tell them someone's taken the sculpture."

Chapter Eight

The call had come late yesterday from Washington MPD, who had responded to Summers' original call about the missing art. They'd been to the bank, checked out the situation, talked to Summers and others—and got nowhere. Nonetheless, as the possible theft involved valuable art, the MPD had requested assistance from the FBI.

As she sat in Peter Summers' office, Wynn Cabot thought it odd that he seemed so nervous when she was only there to help him.

People who are robbed often feel violated, she knew. When the stolen object is not only your responsibility but also the very symbol of your livelihood, well, that might explain his throat-clearing, perspiration, and persistent picking at his cuticles. As he repeated the story about the roof leak, and the need to remove the mobile sculpture, she watched him.

"So you see," Summers' said, "we're naturally curious what happened to Versailles and more importantly, what's become of the *Cornucopia*."

"I imagine you are."

He handed her a leather-bound photo album. "These are photos of the *Cornucopia* as it was being installed. It's a distinct work. A symbol of plenty, with the understanding of more to come."

She leafed through the album quickly. "May I take this with me? I can put all of these photos on the Missing Art Registry."

"Absolutely. We'll want it back when you're done, but keep it as long as you like."

"Anything else you can tell me?

Summers paused and considered another cuticle. "If you're asking do I know who did it, I don't. But I'd bet that one of my ex-employees—a guy named Mark Bowles—set the whole thing up." He stood, signaling the end of the interview. "You'll have our full cooperation, Miss Wynn."

"Cabot. Wynn Cabot."

He held up both hands and gave her a mock smile. "Oh, sorry. Guess I better get that straight if I'm dealing with the FBI."

Wynn turned toward the door before she rolled her eyes, left Summers' office, and returned to the bank lobby to get her bearings. She passed the elevator and went to the center of the floor. The tellers' desks were to her right; the counter with its deposit and withdrawal slips, calendar, and pens on chains to her left. In the far left corner, past the counter, was the front door and just to the right of that, Roybal's guard station with its monitor screens.

She looked down at the shiny marble floor and up at the ceiling, then out the huge windows of bulletproof glass with the UV film that kept the lobby from becoming a big sauna.

Where to start? she wondered.

Her best guess would be to put eyes on the guys who took the sculpture down. She walked to the guard desk.

Roybal stood when he saw her coming, recognizing her from her earlier check-in. "Yes, ma'am, Ms. Cabot?"

"I'm going to need your footage of the day that Versailles came."

"Well, ma'am, that was two days, actually. But like I told the cops, the lobby cameras only look at the tellers' customers."

"There aren't any other cameras?"

"No ma'am, not working. They're just for show. I mean, if we—if Nova Bank was going to be robbed, the tellers would be where it would happen, right?"

"I'll need that footage anyway." She looked out the door. "Were you the one who called Versailles to come?"

"No, ma'am. I believe it was Mr. Bowles. He's a former employee."

"And the day—days—they came, did you help them?"

"Ma'am? Help them what?"

"Did you interact with them in any way?"

Roybal frowned. "Well, I let them in. Mr. Summers told me to make sure the job got done."

"Can you give me a description of them?"

"The main guy, he had this ratty beard." Roybal gave her the description, and she noted it.

"And the tellers? Can they tell me anything?"

Roybal worked his lower jaw. "None of them talked to the guy the first day, and the second day, the tellers weren't here. We were closed."

There was something here, Wynn thought. It might be merely a company that moved offices over the holiday weekend and didn't have their new phone installed yet. But it felt like more.

Leaning on Roybal's desk, she looked at him between two monitors. "What do you think happened here, Mr. Roybal?"

"Ma'am, I have no idea. Ma'am."

Wynn stood in the shade on the steps in front of Nova Bank, wondering if there was anywhere—*anywhere*—in the U.S. that wasn't pressure-cooker hot in July. And if there was, did they have an FBI field office where she might be needed? She removed her suit jacket and folded it over her arm.

She paused, noticing the unmarked government building across the street. No clues to what the building might be. Nothing but a manned guard station, its only distinguishing mark a sign that read, "IDs checked 100%," and above that a closed-circuit camera targeting the driveway that approached the small white hut.

She looked right, to the non-descript office building that sat next to the mysterious government structure. On both upper corners of that building there were closed-circuit cameras as well.

She stepped to the curb, withdrew her credentials from her handbag, threw her jacket in the back seat of the government-issue Ford Focus—or as she had dubbed it the Slow Pocus—and studied the top of the Verizon building that was Nova Bank's immediate neighbor. Lots of cameras. More than were necessary for a telephone switching office.

She watched a large black Cadillac Escalade pull into the driveway of the

Verizon building and disappear around a corner to the back, before she crossed E Street to approach the guard shack of the government building on foot, her Federal ID held high.

"Morning," she said when the guard slid back the window. "FBI. We're investigating something over at Nova Bank."

The guard blinked but said nothing.

"Right. We're going to need to see the footage from your closed-circuit camera there." Wynn pointed to the camera mounted on the corner of the guard shack.

The guard stared at her.

"I'm assuming this is a U.S. government building?"

At last the guard spoke. "It is."

"Who do I talk to about obtaining the camera images from this past weekend?"

"Someone a lot higher than me."

"I can do that," Wynn said.

The guard's glare matched that of Tuesday's midday sun. He slid shut the glass panel on his window and turned away. Wynn waited.

Finally, she rapped a knuckle on the glass.

The guard looked up, but didn't move to open the window a second time.

She got the picture. She returned to the shaded overhang in front of Nova Bank, pulled out her government-issue cell phone and scrolled the numbers until she found the one she sought: Senator Jake Osborne—chair of the Senate Finance Committee.

* * *

Later that day, Osborne returned Wynn's call. He was evasive about the nature of the mysterious government building on E Street. "I know the place," was all he said. "Been in it a time or two."

"What I need," Wynn said, "is a dump of the footage from their guard station for last Thursday."

"Who the hell steals art from a bank, Ms. Cabot?"

"Not stolen, not yet. Missing. Mislaid maybe. You know that mobile that hangs—well, used to hang—in their lobby?"

"Sure. The one that dangles silver and gold doohickies."

"That one. Crew that took it down when the roof leaked last week has ghosted. We need to see what kind of truck they were driving. Oh, and whatever you can give us on Versailles Art Transport would help too. You know, corporate officers, location, that kind of thing."

"The closed-circuit images will be on a hard drive—I can have them dump that day to a thumb drive for you."

"That'd be fine—I just need the footage from last Friday, June 19. And try to hurry it along every chance you get, Senator. Oh—and can you find us corporate info on Versailles?"

"Can't you? Sure you can. That's easy stuff."

"I have a hunch there'll be no company officers listed, don't you?"

Osborne sighed. "No, probably not. Not if they're a sham, which is what this feels like. Look, I hesitate to pierce the corporate veil on anybody until I have to. Let's see first if you can find the sculpture without it. I'll have my aide get on that thumb drive request first thing tomorrow. The doing of it, that's another matter. It'll take a week or so, by the time it's requested, approved, done, and sent over to you."

Wynn leaned back in her desk chair and thought—what had she learned? What did she have? Footage, photographs and a feeling. Something was too convenient about the fact that the guy who hired the transport company had resigned suddenly, that almost nobody worked the day they came, that everybody paused a little too long before they answered any questions.

If they answered the questions at all.

The guard in the shack across the street hadn't been forthcoming with help.

Metropolitan Police would send over all the surveillance tape they had, which they said wasn't much, and she thought that odd for one of the most surveilled sites in D.C., a block that housed an MPD sub-station. A piece was missing there.

She looked at the art removal company's business card, clipped to the front of the case folder.

She heard an electric chime and wondered at its source for a moment before she realized it had come from her disposable phone. Digging in her purse, she found the phone and checked the screen, almost yelping aloud when she saw she had a text:

Did not know if you had seen

And a link to an article in the *Wall Street Journal*'s European Edition. Its title read:

U.S. Carrier Stennis in Eastern Med

She smiled. Bishop was on that ship. On his way home.

Chapter Nine

Seamus Caine saw Wynn's name and number in the readout on his phone and his spirits rose. He heard from her more often now that she was on the east coast, but each call still delighted him. She had once been his protégé and a rising star in the firmament of Caine et Cie, Fine Art Appraisers. When she'd left the firm to go to work for the FBI, he'd moped in her absence. He loved what precious little time he could spend talking to her, although he knew if she called midday as she was doing now, she needed information.

After pleasantries, she got to the point. "What can you tell me about fine art transport?"

"What is it you want to move?"

"Not me." She filled him in on the disappearance of the mobile sculpture from the bank. "What do you think—genuine theft, or legitimate company gone radio silent for a few days?"

Leaning back in his leather wing chair in the library of his Back Bay Boston mansion, Caine rested his elbow on the arm of the chair, draping his free hand over his considerable middle. "Art transport is common sense, only more so. If you want to send Aunt Hilda's portrait back to the cousins, you can take it to a pack-and-ship store, and it'll probably be fine. They'll wrap it and ship it and give you a tracking number to see that it got there."

"This was a bit more than that, Seamus."

"Quite so. In this case, one would call upon a company whose business is the transport of fine art—though some wonderful companies are offshoots of other businesses—display companies or moving-and-storage outfits. But a truly reputable art transport firm, no matter its, well, parentage, will have procedures and equipment to do a careful and secure job."

"The bank guard made it sound like they had all the bells and whistles. And were careful."

"When they came, did they take photos?"

"The guard says they did."

"Did they take photos as they took the work down and wrapped it?"

"I didn't ask." She made a note to do that.

"Did someone get the photos sent to them? Or a link to a website?"

"I'll find out."

"Did the company wear gloves while they handled the work? As they took it down and wrapped it, did they label the bundles? What did they wrap it in?"

"Felt bags and moving blankets, the guard said."

"But no moisture barrier."

"Actually, it had already got wet." She told him about the ceiling leak at the bank.

"Moving on, then, so to speak. Was this piece mixed in with other art?"

"Oh, this is sounding worse and worse."

"What kind of truck did they use? Did it have air-ride suspension?"

"What does that do?"

"They replace the vehicle's springs with, essentially, air bags. It keeps the cargo from being damaged by shock or vibration. Was the truck secure? Did it have GPS? Did the drivers have Threat Assessment Training?"

"It's a sculpture."

"It's worth a lot of money. Where did they take the piece, do you know?"

"We do not."

"Domestically, it's easier to move over state lines, or in your case, District lines. Internationally, there are reams of paperwork to fill out—permits, dispensations, carnets. Otherwise, you're basically...smuggling."

"So it's harder to move internationally, and harder to find domestically. It could be anywhere." Wynn closed her eyes for a moment. "I don't think this one's left the country. Not yet, anyway."

40

"Still, wherever they took it needs to be climate-controlled and secure, with limited access and some kind of retrieval system—those warehouses can be huge. And more moisture barrier, in case a sprinkler system goes off. Some places, if you want, you can have a padded cell all to yourself. Which sounds tempting sometimes, when the world is too much with us."

"You could never live in a padded cell."

"Not if it kept me away from you, darling. Come and see me, soon."

"I will," she promised.

No sooner had she ended the call than the chime sounded on her phone and a text message popped onto the screen: Good thing I have Prudential Insurance

She Googled the venerable company, and nodded when the logo came up on her screen: The Rock of Gibraltar, where she knew the U.S. maintained a substantial military presence.

Bishop must be in Spain, she thought. Well, that was progress, but she wished he'd hurry.

Chapter Ten

Mark Bowles and the single-minded Mrs. Bowles lived in a small but toney condo in the middle of D.C., a short walk from Logan Circle and close enough to Nova Bank that it had been a brief ride to his former job.

His new job would be in the heart of suburban Virginia, in a glass and stucco building whose directory did not list FinCEN—the United States' Financial Crimes Enforcement Network, an arm of the Treasury Department. Bowles's commute to this final job interview wasn't a short one.

On Thursday, June 25th, Mark Bowles dressed in his best bankers' gray pinstripes, a white shirt and red rep tie, checked to be sure the manila file containing the Suspicious Activities Reports was in his briefcase, and took an Uber to FinCEN's Chain Bridge Road address in Vienna, Virginia.

Bowles had been working with FinCEN's Enforcement Division for a number of months, filing reports on suspicious activities he'd observed at Nova Bank. The single manila file now in his briefcase was the one he'd maintained and kept in his safe-deposit box, and it contained copies of each of those reports. Now, he was going to work for the investigators themselves, as their new Public Affairs Coordinator.

He expected to meet first with FinCEN's Director, his new boss, who would review the mission statement and the agency's position within the financial community and how Bowles should position it. After that, of course, he would be handed off to someone from Human Resources who would have him fill out the usual tax forms and 401K info, and then show him around and introduce him to co-workers.

He was prepared, dressed appropriately, and knew he was the right candidate for the job. When he stepped off the elevator he was met by a young woman who worked in Security, packed the heat to prove it, and did her smart navy blue uniform and stiletto heels great justice. She escorted Bowles across a room full of open work-stations to an empty conference room, told him to have a seat and shut the door, leaving him alone in the room.

Bowles laid his briefcase on the conference room table, snapped open the latches, withdrew the manila folder, opened it, and gasped. Instead of copies of incriminating Suspicious Activities Reports—his insurance that Peter Summers and Howard Jacobs would eventually go to jail for embezzlement and money laundering—he saw only pages from old phone books and Sunday comics. Gone were the Suspicious Activity Reports accusing Peter Summers of fraud, photos of Summers in compromising situations with women other than his wife, emails Summers had written using anti-Semitic language when discussing the Jacobses, and others describing some of the tellers in plainly sexist and often salacious terms.

All of it, gone.

Of course, FinCEN would have their copies of the SARs Bowles had filed with them over the past couple of years. But the photos and emails—who had those? What had happened between the last time he'd put something in that file and locked it back in his safe-deposit box at Nova Bank, and last Wednesday, when he removed the file for the final time?

The conference room door opened and two men stepped into the room, neither of whom he recognized as the FinCEN's Director, Keith Barrett. One, a flush-faced younger man, stepped forward.

"Mr. Bowles? I'm John Byrne, Assistant to the Director. He...uh, we, understand you thought you might work here?"

Bowles blinked. "Might? That was my understanding from the interview last week."

"Yes, well, that has changed. We'd like you to keep your job at Nova Bank for the near term and—"

"That's not possible. I've resigned. Summers had me walked out. You—that is, FinCEN—offered me the position of Public Affairs Coordinator. I accepted."

Byrne shrugged. "There was nothing on paper, was there? Nothing in writing."

"Your Human Resources person—"

"—got ahead of herself in offering you the job. Is there any way you can go back to Nova?"

"No."

"Well, I'm sorry it didn't work out here. But we've filled the Public Affairs position in the meantime. Have a good day."

"Have a good day? *Have a—*"

Byrne sighed and turned to the man behind him. "Tell him."

An ashen-faced older man stepped forward, his voice soft and unhurried. "We're both with the Office of Special Measures here. FinCEN has had a breach of files—we don't know how. The SARs you sent us have been taken. That is, they're no longer...they've disappeared."

Bowles dropped into a chair, propped his elbows on the conference table and pressed his palms to his forehead. "As have my copies. I checked just now."

Byrne sat opposite Bowles, but said nothing.

Bowles opened his briefcase again, pulled out the file folder and opened it to display the sheet of Sunday comics on top. Byrne riffled the pages and then chucked the folder in a nearby wastebasket. "Come with me. I think something can be worked out."

Chapter Eleven

With a quiet word to the tellers, Peter Summers closed the bank—a privilege he could invoke from time to time because of the bank's "boutique" status and just for special customers—and instructed Roybal to stand guard and wait. Congressman B. Crawford Dawson was due at four o'clock.

So Roybal stood guard and waited. Two people tried the door, but he waved them off, pointing to the CLOSED sign, calling to one through the door that she should use the ATM a few yards away.

Finally a limousine rolled to the curb, the driver got out, and opened the door for his passenger. The man was shorter than he looked on TV, but his look was unmistakable: longish silver hair and a Buffalo Bill mustache and beard.

As the man neared the door, Roybal stooped to undo the first of the locks, the deadbolt that went into the door sill. Then he turned back the bolt at the door handle. Finally, he swiped his own key card through a reader on the nearby wall, entered a code on the keypad. When the keypad lights turned green, he opened the door to admit Summers' guest.

Summers came across the lobby to greet the man. "Billy, you are a sight for sore eyes," he said, shaking the man's hand. "Come on in. I'll pour us some bourbon and branch and we'll bang ears for a spell."

Congressman B. Crawford Dawson rolled his eyes. "Good lord, Summers," he said in his plummy Carolina drawl, "this place looks as empty as the Sugar Bowl after the Bulldogs beat Baylor. And look at this floor. Dammit to hell, Summers, we paid good money for your prissy floor. What the hell happened?"

"Oh, this, it's just a hiccup." Summers waved Roybal away, dismissing the wet, rusty mess on the marble floor with a wave of a hand. "A little rain damage. We've had repairmen in."

Dawson looked up at the new paint on the high, arched ceiling. "I'm sure that was a big bill."

"Spoken like a true member of our board of directors, Billy. Don't worry, insurance will pay for it, believe me. And I surely hope Jacobs's policy covers the damage to the *Cornucopia* as well." Summers studied the streaks of white on the Congressman's neck, where his spray tan hadn't made it into the creases.

Dawson looked at the ceiling for another long moment, then lowered his gaze to take in the lobby, and finally looked at Roybal as though he saw the security guard for the first time.

"Yes," he said, distracted. "Of course."

"...and so, of course," Summers said as he handed Dawson a neat two fingers of Blanton's in a Baccarat old fashioned glass, "while we'll get something in the way of insurance money for the sculpture, it won't be enough."

Dawson sipped and nodded. He leaned back in one of the leather button-tufted wing chairs that flanked Summers' desk and sipped again. "That's damned fine bourbon, Peter."

"A gift from Frank Underwood, before he...left office. The short-fall, Billy? What do we do?"

Dawson thought and then caught his breath. *Sometimes, Dawson,* he thought, *you are smarter than people give you credit for.* "I've met someone I think can help us. You don't need to know any more than that. Let me put this together. We should be made whole by the end of the month." He tossed back the bourbon and stood. "And then no more of this horse-shit, y'hear?"

Wynn Cabot's burner phone chimed and a text came up. This time the message from Bishop was more cryptic:

I haven't feltwell in days

No doubt that was true, she thought. To travel with a wound like his would require a resilience she knew he had, but wished he didn't have to use. On

46

and off ships, probably in and out of ambulances, helicopters, stretching, jostling. It hurt to think about.

But—wait. Was the misspelling deliberate? She searched the Net for feltwell. Yes, there it was—Feltwell. A town in England. A town with a big U.S. Air Force Base.

André Bishop mashed on the red call button again and then tossed the call unit aside and looked out his hospital room window.

His room, while not exactly at Feltwell, was next door at Lakenheath, the RAF base that the U.S. Air Force shares with the U.K. He jerked his head away from the window and gulped back homesickness. To that he added shame that he'd become a drain on the system—he'd been moved from place to place by fine first responders, people who had better things to do than jerk his pathetic bones from ship to aircraft to ambulance and then the reverse time and time again, and would be still until they got him home.

Grabbing the call unit again, he squeezed the button with both thumbs. He realized he was a guest in this facility, but couldn't someone bring him something for the pain?

He clenched the call unit in his fist. How the hell had he even put himself in a situation where he might get shot? Hadn't he promised himself after the first time...

And that was the problem, wasn't it? Years ago, tailing an arms dealer through what Bishop thought was the "nicer" part of Tampa, he'd taken a bullet in the leg that tore muscle and nicked bone. Afterward, quickly and quietly, he was transferred from Criminal Division to Art Crimes. The physical damage was a telltale scar, an ache during bad weather, and an inability to juke on a basketball court. But his psyche suffered the most lasting damage: a reluctance to take target practice, which was getting better, and hating the sight of blood, which wasn't.

Oh, he'd screwed up good this time, no doubt about it. And now there was Wynn Cabot to add to the mix. If he dropped communication with her, she might do something foolish to try to find him.

If he could force himself to think, to concentrate on the Jerusalem case, he might make some sense out of what happened that night, and salvage something out of all of this. Problem was, there were big black gaps in his memory, not only what happened that night but also the whole case. His files had been left at the hotel, to be retrieved by Israeli agents and maybe, someday, returned to him. Unfortunately, all he could summon to his consciousness right now was the knowledge that it must have involved priceless art being smuggled to the U.S.

Still, there was more, hiding in a locker in his brain, the combination obscured by pain and the trauma of being shot again. There were secrets, and double crosses, and someone's name...

An orderly appeared by his bed.

Time to move again.

Chapter Twelve

As she'd promised she would, Wynn waited a couple of days until Friday to circle back to MPD to hear their findings. She called the substation and caught officer Julie "Frosty" Winters as she was coming off shift.

"Afraid there's not much to tell you, Cabot."

"You were going to run prints, sweepings, maybe some DNA."

"We did. And got nothing. Nothing in the floor sweepings but plaster scraps. DNA takes six weeks minimum when we have a good sample, which we don't here."

"Prints?"

"The construction repair crew cut out and re-plastered that whole section of the arch, and hauled off the trash. If any of the Versailles guys touched it, it's long gone now."

"Other surfaces? Did you—"

"Cabot, listen. We got muggings, rapes, and a couple murders here. We can't give missing artwork a whole lot of time without something concrete to go on." Winters paused. "Sorry. This one's all yours."

Wynn rubbed her forehead. "Okay, then, get me your files."

"You can have everything. Someone will drop it off ASAP."

Wynn ended the call and moped. She would have to grind it out the old-fashioned way, as Bishop would say, with a lot of phone calls and leg work and fingers crossed for a lucky break.

But Bishop wasn't here, and she was on her own. Well, not really on her own, she thought, but under the scrutiny of her boss's boss. And Wynn wanted to look good for the top brass, wanted to prove that she could wade her way through the boring day-to-day scut work to come up with the gem that would solve the case.

It was time, she knew, to put on her jeans and go get dirty.

Summers responded to her doing more digging with even less warmth this time. "What the hell do you want to dig in our trash for? The police already did that and found nothing." His voice echoed around the lobby.

"Which is why the police turned it over to the FBI. I'll be as unobtrusive as I can, I promise. But this is not a request."

He waved her off, turned on his heel, and headed for his office. Wynn pivoted and made for Roybal's guard desk.

When he looked up, she said, "Tell me again about the day Versailles was here."

"Yes, ma'am. They got here about nine, brought in a bunch of pressboard, and taped it to the floor. Then they brought in a personnel lift and took the thing, the sculpture, down. Then they left."

"Show me where they put the pressboard down."

Roybal walked her along the route from the door to the point beneath where the mobile had hung. Twice, she dropped to her knees, hoping she'd get lucky and find tape residue with a fingerprint in it. But when she knelt a third time, he said, "Ma'am? You won't find anything. This floor was washed and buffed Monday morning before we opened. To clean up the construction mess."

She put her cheek on the floor to look across the surface. The floor shone smooth and flawless, a mirror for the work of art that should have hung above them.

"Okay," she said, rising. "So then they brought in a man-lift. How big?"

"Four wheels, with a scissor lift. Almost as wide as the door."

Her head snapped around, and she bolted for the door. "Did they chock the door? Did one of them hold it?"

Roybal wet his lips. "I held it for them. And the door, all of the glass, really, has been cleaned since then."

"Ah. And none of them touched anything?"

"They wore gloves. To protect the sculpture, they said."

"Did they leave anything? A receipt for the mobile, a claim check, a business card?"

"A card. But I think you have that."

Letting Roybal return to his desk, Wynn retrieved her evidence-collection kit—useless now that there was no evidence.

She heard the signal from her Walmart phone.

The text from Bishop's number read:

Thinking about a dog. Black lab maybe

Of course, she thought. He's in Labrador. Made it to North America. Pleased and buoyed by Bishop's progress, she chucked the phone in her bag.

Time to hit the trash bin.

She'd only Dumpster dived twice in this job, barfing the first time, but not the second. But she couldn't imagine there would be much smelly garbage in a bank trash bin, would there? The odd lunch scraps, maybe, expired salad dressing from the office fridge? How bad could it be? Swinging open the corrugated plastic lid, she stood on tiptoe to peer inside.

The bin was almost empty. Obviously, the trash had been picked up recently. Still, she had to check.

With her muscular arms, she hoisted herself up on the rim of the bin, swung her legs over the side and dropped in. The bottom was wet from the recent rain, but the items were fairly dry. Snapping on latex gloves, she catalogued the contents: two cups and a bag from the Capitol Café down the street, a book of completed Sudoku puzzles, pages from a legal pad, covered with ballpoint stripes and swirls. No doubt from a "bored" meeting, she thought.

In the bottom of the bin, stuck to the floor with the rancid, rusty rainwater, sparkled specks of silver and gold glitter. She considered it for a moment, dismissed it as left over from a June graduation celebration, and climbed out of the bin.

She looked down at her new Converse All-Stars. They'd never be the same. She'd sacrificed them for nothing. Stripping off her gloves, she tossed them into the bin. She wasn't done yet, not by any stretch.

Right now, though, she needed a weekend off.

And garbage or no garbage, she needed a shower.

Chapter Thirteen

By Monday morning, Wynn felt as clear and bright as the weather, ready to face the tasks ahead of her. She'd slept well over the weekend, run errands and grocery shopped, and had twice been to the YMCA for lengthy swims.

On Saturday, the pool's lifeguard had approached her. "You swim well," he'd said. "Real well."

"Thanks."

"No, seriously, you could compete."

"I used to. Now I swim for the exercise."

"Actually, I wanted to ask…would you consider…"

Here it comes, she thought. First the flattery, then the awkward come-on.

"…maybe teaching? Helping out with the kids?"

Wynn was confounded. She'd been wrong about him and his motives. "Oh. I wish I could. I've got a job that's more than full-time right now."

"Maybe you could teach a master class. A one-off, on stroke mechanics or something. Just say you'll think about it."

She wrung the towel over the edge of the pool. "Yeah. I'll think about it."

"'K. Hey, tell me your name."

Turning to go, she smiled and called over her shoulder, "Wynn Cabot." She didn't see his eyes widen, or his jaw drop.

"You're Wynn Cabot? *The* Wynn Cabot? Hey, I saw you on TV—"

She waved a hand and disappeared into the ladies' locker room.

Halfway through the Monday, though, her mood began to flag and no amount of coffee—certainly not the office joe—could lift her out of it. She

53

hadn't heard from Bishop all weekend and wanted to know where he was, that he was progressing not only in terms of his trip home, but also in his physical recovery. She checked her burner phone for texts. Nothing.

And working on the Nova Bank case was no more productive. Ending her thirteenth call on a list of twenty-three, she dialed the next number just as Grazer appeared at her desk and plopped into Wynn's guest chair.

"Here's the deal," Grazer said. "I need to know where you are with this."

Good morning to you, too, Wynn thought, and filled Grazer in on what she had—and didn't have—so far. "I got the file from MPD this morning, but it's skinny. So I left a message with the construction company, telling them that I want to interview the crew. And I've tried all morning to find an equipment rental company that rented out a man-lift that weekend. So far, everybody got the big kind, for outdoor use."

"Keep me advised," Grazer said, and leaned in. "I want to know what you're up to."

"Yes, ma'am." Wynn's mouth went dry. Did Grazer know about Wynn's finding and tracking Bishop? Could she have found out?

Grazer left. Wynn took her handbag from the bottom drawer of her desk, quietly shut the drawer and left the office.

Wynn climbed out of her car, frowned at the GPS map on her phone, and checked her notes again: yes, this was the address on the Versailles business card. Or it might have been, had there actually been offices or storage facilities or something, anything besides…

Grave markers.

The address on the card was for Oak Hill Cemetery. A fact she could have found out on her computer, she thought, had she taken a minute to follow the GPS directions to the arrival point. That's probably what the cops had done and saved themselves a trip over here.

At least she'd had the foresight to have the telephone number researched, rather than calling it for the umpteenth time and expecting someone to answer. The number had never belonged to Versailles. It wasn't temporarily or mistakenly disconnected. It was a hoax.

She had checked the website and email on the card too. Both of those were fakes.

And Frosty Winters at MPD had said there were plenty of fingerprints on the card—Roybal's, Summers' and Jacobs'—but no unknowns.

Her disposable cell phone chimed. She snatched it from her handbag and thumbed the text icon.

The message read: *Medical Exam. Can't Talk*

She pursed her lips and wondered exactly where Bishop could be that he was getting a medical exam. Was he still in Labrador? At a hospital there? Was everything okay? Checking the text again, she noted the capital letters, and reminded herself that they could be deliberate. She separated them:

ME. CT.

Maine. Connecticut. He was getting closer.

Heaving a sigh of relief, she got back in the car, grateful for its meager air conditioning, swung a U, and headed to her afternoon interview.

Unlike Versailles Art Transport, Phelps Construction did exist. Wynn leaned on a counter top and talked to the crew who sat in beat-up plastic chairs, their feet propped on a three-legged coffee table. Narville Phelps—a tall, muscular man, she noted—examined the soles of his work boots while she asked her questions.

"No," he said, "we never saw the guys who took the sculpture down. I'm not sure what we can tell you."

"Did they leave any tools?"

"They didn't leave any anything. My guys here, they used ladders to access the exterior, up on the roof. But inside, we even had to lay our own pressboard, bring in our own scaffolding."

"You didn't see their vehicle?"

Phelps shook his head, peeling something off his boot and flicking it to the floor.

"And I don't suppose you saved any of the ceiling?"

He guffawed. "That stuff? From wet sheetrock to roofing, all of it was a real mess. Went straight to the dump."

Which is where this case may be headed, she thought, because coming at it via the bank was getting her nowhere.

She needed a new angle.

Chapter Fourteen

Last Thursday, John Byrne, FinCEN's Special Measures hotshot, had assured Mark Bowles that they would find a spot for him "somewhere in the agency." And then he'd walked Bowles to the elevator, pushed the Down button, and said again, "Have a good day."

"We'll be in touch, Mr. Bowles," Bowles muttered as the elevator doors shut. "We look forward to working with you, Mr. Bowles. Don't let the door hit you in the ass on your way out, Mr. Bowles."

But on Friday, an obsequious Byrne called Bowles to say FinCEN's Special Measures group wanted another meeting—they understood he had further information they wanted to see. They would send a car for him at ten Monday morning.

Bowles was wary after the Thursday visit had blown up in his face, but no one else was interested in even glancing at his CV right now. Being unemployed prolonged being unemployed. He had nothing to lose.

It wasn't costing him the price of an Uber ride, he'd already worked out at the Y that morning, and he had the rest of the day on his hands. Once again he dressed in a summer-weight gray flannel suit, went to the small safe he kept in his home office, spun the dial for the four-digit combination, and withdrew an envelope.

He checked to see if the envelope's contents still existed. After he'd been fooled by his CYA folder's bogus fill, he'd be more careful. Yes, there it was—a single sheet of paper, with more damning information than he needed on the people who needed to be damned for what they'd done to him. He tucked the envelope into an inside jacket pocket.

A black Lincoln Town Car pulled to the curb at exactly ten a.m. and the same security guard he'd seen the week before, in her navy blue uniform and four-inch stiletto heels jumped out, walked to the rear curb-side door, opened it and waited for Bowles to emerge from his condo.

Bowles settled into the back seat and the young woman expertly jockeyed the car out of D.C.'s mid-morning traffic and across the Potomac River, where she picked up U.S. 66.

An odd choice of route, Bowles thought. He leaned forward and tapped a finger on the driver's seat. "This faster than the Parkway?"

"I thought this way best," she said.

"Ah. Oh. I see." Bowles sat back, studying cars and commuter trains, and beyond them, left and right, a sea of bedroom communities shimmering in the warm late-June morning.

The driver, a trim brunette with high cheekbones, didn't make conversation, nor did the Town Car's radio play NPR's *Midday Edition*.

Bowles glanced at his phone and frowned: 10:30 a.m. They should be arriving at FinCEN any minute, but they were nowhere near the Tyson's Corners retail mess that surrounded the headquarters building.

He studied road signs for a clue as to where exactly they were in relation to FinCEN's Chain Bridge Road address and took in a breath. FinCEN was a good ten minutes north, and the driver had just passed the last exit that headed that way.

He checked the car's back doors. Locked. He felt for a door-lock button but fingered, instead, a small metal plate that might cover a disabled lock mechanism from being operated in the back seat. He'd been childproofed.

His greater fear, as the Town Car moved west on 66 past Fairfax, now, and toward Centreville, was that he was being kidnapped. He pulled out his phone again. 10:40 a.m. And no signal.

He glanced around the car, looking for a cell-signal jammer, and then shook his head. Jamming devices were the size of a button now, and something that small could be hidden anywhere in the car. Anywhere.

He cleared his throat. "The FinCEN building is in Tyson's Corners, right?"

"So far as I know," the driver said.

"Didn't we pass the turnoff back there?"

"We're not going to FinCEN."

"Weren't you sent by John Byrne?"

"Look, Mr. Bowles," she said without taking her eyes from the road, "I have a job to do, which I believe, right now, is more than what you have. I was given an address and that's where we're going."

"How much longer until we get there?"

The driver looked at her cell phone. "About another hour."

"Another *hour*? Where are we going?"

She looked over her shoulder at him and smiled. "Why don't you sit back and enjoy the ride? You'll find out soon enough."

Bedroom communities gave way to rolling pasture-land and horse country, and the Town Car lofted along in cushy silence.

"I have no cell service, you know," Bowles said.

"Right."

"Any reason why not?"

"If it makes you feel any better, I don't have cell service in the car either."

Bowles sat back in the seat again and thought. He'd find out in an hour what this was about. In the meantime, maybe he should enjoy just being alive. It might not last.

Executive kidnappings still happened, he knew, especially kidnappings of bankers, but no one talked about it much anymore. Much of it occurred overseas or in Latin American countries. Most of it for ransom, which was paid after some negotiating. And then the executive was released, and that was that.

Bowles wouldn't be worth anything as a kidnap victim, he knew, except for the contents of the envelope in his pocket. If kidnapping was in the cards today, then with a little duct tape around his wrists, the kidnappers could get to the envelope even before they made a ransom request. But there was no bank to which kidnappers might make a ransom demand—he wasn't valuable to anyone right now. Not having the contents of the envelope would make him worthless and being worthless was worse than being held for ransom.

But whoever got hold of the envelope and the letter within would be in bad shape too, unless it was the letter's author or its recipient. The author, Summers, wasn't the kidnapper type—he had too much to lose in status if he got caught—and he would get caught; he wasn't smart enough not to. The letter's recipient didn't give a shit about image or people, which made him even less a suspect. He doubted he'd find either of them at the end of this trip.

At precisely 12:15 p.m. the Lincoln Town Car pulled up in front of the main building at the Inn at Little Washington. The driver put the car in Park, sprang from the front seat and marched almost militarily to open the door for Bowles.

As he climbed out, relief washed over him. No ominous figures in black balaclavas waited to hogtie him—indeed he hadn't been kidnapped at all, he'd been taken to one of the most exclusive restaurants in the D.C. area. He looked up to see John Byrne and FinCEN's Director, Keith Barrett, waiting on The Inn's veranda.

The three of them sat in the kitchen, at a table usually reserved for celebrities of various sorts, or those who wished to remain unrecognized, even though no one sat at the main dining room's elegant tables. The Inn at Little Washington had made an unusual exception for these men and served them lunch. The din of chefs preparing the evening meal rang behind them.

"Look," Barrett said over dessert and coffee, "we had hoped you could help from inside. When we need eyes somewhere, you would be sent in. Special Measures sometimes uses people who…shall we say, freelance."

Bowles nodded. "I can do that, and I'd be glad to. But I'll need a salary. A steady income, rather than free-lance, piece-meal payments."

"I can assure you, you'd make more working by the job than on salary," Byrne said.

"That may be, but you," Bowles cocked an eyebrow at Director Barrett, "assured me I had a full-time position at FinCEN—until I didn't."

Barrett nodded. "Then here's what we'll do—you can have the salary we initially agreed upon, contingent on our seeing all of the letters you intercepted when you sign on. But first I want to see the one you brought today."

Bowles withdrew the envelope from his jacket pocket, inhaled deeply, and handed it to Barrett.

The director studied it intently and then handed it to Byrne, who glanced it over and gasped. "This is off-shore transfers—not out of the country, but in."

Bowles nodded. "There are more. Twenty in all. Different accounts on the transfer end, each from various countries, but always to the same account here in D.C."

"Then the missing SARs are irrelevant, aren't they?" Barrett said. "We have the sources for them."

Byrne stirred his coffee and then raised his spoon. "Irrelevant maybe, but I want to know who took them."

Marlene Reese had just arrived at home when her cell phone rang. She looked at the readout and shook her head: B Dawson. Was he really dumb enough to use his own name to call someone like "Polly?" She picked up the call just before it rolled to voicemail. "Polly here."

"Got a situation I need your help with."

"My help, Congressman?"

"Yes, well, let me put it this way—if you don't help, I might let some folks down at Nova

Bank know about the conversation we had last week."

"You didn't let them know last week, why would you say something now?"

"I thought I might wait until I needed to use you for something."

"Go ahead."

"Polly, I need for you to get into those safe-deposit boxes again. In exchange for returning the ledgers you took from my box."

She chuckled. "You want me to give you back those ledgers *and* do you a favor?"

"You think I put the only copy of the books in that box, do you?"

"Then why the burning desire to get what I have back?"

"If you push me, I'll prove you stole those ledgers and don't think I won't. That was a dumb move on your part, Polly—to take them and let me know you have them. Kind of makes you a target for a lot of…inventive things."

Silence on both ends of the line.

She smiled to herself. Congressman B. Crawford Dawson wasn't as smart as she'd thought. She could make her own copies, just as he had. She lifted her chin and said, "Fine. Deal. I'll mail them tomorrow. To your office. What do you want me to do?"

"Our mutual friend needs some more ready cash."

She sighed. This situation was getting tiresome, but it would be over soon. "In the first place, he's your friend, not mine."

"He's your—"

"And in the second place," she said, "I have a better idea. Have you ever heard of a 'double whammy'?"

"In the general sense, yes."

"You'll need to assemble a team. But here's how it works…"

Chapter Fifteen

On Monday night James Roybal's tiny studio apartment was dim and close in the summer heat. Staring at the notebook screen on his coffee table, Roybal struggled to stay awake. He didn't mind having to take the written exam to be considered for the Metropolitan Police Department, but the stinking practice exams were a mind-numbing bore. Roybal figured if he ever had insomnia, he knew the exact web pages he could turn to for a sleep aid.

A knock on the door jolted his eyes open.

He checked the peephole, but as a twenty-eight-year-old Army veteran and body builder, Roybal wasn't afraid of two guys in pinstriped suits—guys he recognized—standing in the hall. One of them had a frame like his own; Roybal recalled him as the limo driver from the previous Thursday afternoon. He was now obviously serving as muscle for the other man, Congressman B. Crawford Dawson.

He opened the door. Dawson looked up at him and put a finger to his lips. Silently Roybal stepped back to let the two men enter his small apartment, then scanned the hallway to see if anyone else had seen who was calling on him at almost midnight. Seeing no one, he closed the door and turned to his caller.

"What are you doing here?"

"Thank you for seeing me," Dawson said. "May we sit?"

Roybal refused to be flustered. A Congressman, here in his own apartment, well, that was like dealing with the top brass on base. He took a stack of magazines from the couch and toed two dumbbells from the center of the floor to a corner. Satisfied, he motioned to the others to sit.

Dawson sat. "Sam will wait by the door," he said.

Sam took his place.

"Can I get you something?" Roybal asked. "Water, or some juice? I don't keep liquor. Don't drink."

"I know. Please sit, Mr. Roybal," Dawson said. "When I said 'we' I didn't mean it royally."

The Congressman's words made the hair on his neck stand at attention. Lowering himself to the bed across from the couch, Roybal listened as Dawson spoke low, slow and even.

"Mr. Roybal, I'll come straight to the point. Meeting you last week, I thought I might visit tonight to inquire if you'd be interested in helping out with a matter," he leaned forward, "of national security."

Roybal leaned forward to match. "I'm always down with helping my country."

"Good, good. Because you see, James—may I call you James?—it has come to the attention of... persons at the highest levels that there are, let's just say, items being stored at Nova Bank that could compromise the integrity of America's defense."

Roybal's mind swam. Why had Dawson not shared this with Summers? Or had he? Why was he including a security guard in his...endeavor to save the country, or whatever it was that was going on? "Like, in someone's office? Or in the vault?"

"Like in a safe deposit box." Dawson put his elbows on his knees. "And the timing is getting to be such that we need to recover those items into the possession of the United States in such a way that first—" here Dawson held up a thumb—"they are delivered into our safekeeping. And second—" keeping his thumb up, he unfolded his index finger—"the person who stored the items is drawn out and exposed as a, well, as a terrorist." He leveled the index finger at Roybal and made a shooting gesture. "Are you with me?"

Bewildered, Roybal shot to his feet, prompting the muscle at the door to spring into a fight-ready stance. Dawson held up a hand to stay the watchdog and kept his eyes on Roybal.

Roybal ruffled his hair, put his hands on his hips and paced the tiny room. He had a couple questions, not the least of which was the legality of what Dawson was asking. "I don't know, Congressman, I—"

"Call me Billy. Everyone who knows me does."

"You're talking about a robbery, aren't you?"

"I'm talking about a clandestine government operation to recover sensitive materials."

"But I can't let a heist occur on my watch. I've applied to the MPD." He waved at the tablet on the coffee table.

"I know that too," Dawson said again, "and your exams are coming up."

Of course he would know, Roybal thought. There are no secrets any more. "But if I let the bank get robbed, I—"

"We'll handle MPD," Dawson assured him, "if that's what you want. We'll make it look like you did everything you could…" He stood. "…for your country. For the safety of the American people."

He clapped a hand on Roybal's shoulder, but had to reach up to do it. "I know you did your tour of duty already, but this is Reveille on the most important day of your service."

Roybal's shoulders sagged as if under the weight of Dawson's hand. "What do I have to do?"

Dawson moved toward the door. "Sam will deliver precise instructions to you." He thrust out his hand to shake Roybal's. "And son, I give you the sincere thanks of a grateful nation."

Chapter Sixteen

I n the E Street heat, on Tuesday the thirtieth, Wynn began a canvass of the office buildings in the neighborhood around the bank. She figured someone might have seen something—either on the sidewalk or from a window on a higher floor—around the removal of the sculpture. She knew she'd have to find, and question, as many people as she could.

That was a long shot, and getting longer. The mobile had been taken down on Friday the nineteenth, eleven days ago. To find someone, anyone, who'd made a note of bundles being loaded into an inconspicuous panel truck, was a needle in a haystack after almost two weeks, and Wynn knew it.

That morning, she'd picked up a batch of fliers from the printing office:

Did You See Suspicious Activity
Regarding a white panel van on this block
Friday, June 19th?
Did you see a license plate?
Can you describe the person or persons you saw
In or around the truck?
THE FBI WANTS YOUR HELP
Please email

…with the email address printed at the bottom. *Best I can do right now*, she thought.

Knowing the guy in the government building guard shack was a man of few words, she let that one go. She'd have her security-cam footage soon enough, thanks to Jake Osborne, and that would do for input from that quarter.

Turning next to the office building at 30 E Street, she pushed open the door and headed for the Information desk where three broad-shouldered men with bulges in their armpits sat behind a horseshoe-shaped counter.

"Hi," she said to the one in the middle, and flashed her badge. "Wynn Cabot, FBI. I wonder if I can speak to the tenants of your building, regarding a crime last—"

"No," he said.

"No?"

"In order to gain access to an office here, you need to have an appointment."

Rats, she thought. "So, in order to speak to each of the tenants…"

"You need to have an appointment with each of the tenants."

She'd figured it would be something like this. "Okay," she said, "I have some fliers here. Can I just leave these, and you can make them available for the folks upstairs?" Flashing a bright smile, she set part of her stack of fliers on the horseshoe.

"Certainly." He returned her smile.

"Thanks." Patting the counter, she smiled again and left the lobby.

The security guard watched her go. The moment she was out the door, he scooped the fliers off the curved counter and tossed them in the trash.

Outside, an electronic tone signaled from deep within Wynn's purse.

She pulled out the burner phone and read the text:

Much more of this and I'll need a mask and wig

Mask and wig? she thought. *He's going incognito? Under cover?*

A quick Internet search led to the answer: The Mask and Wig Club. Bishop was in Philadelphia.

B. Crawford Dawson leaned back in his chair, steepled his hands, and thought about his dream team. The first member was Dawson himself—the only one who knew where to find each of the members, and who they really were.

He had his locksmith—the way into the safe-deposit vault, and the boxes themselves—a woman he knew as Polly.

And now he had Roybal, the bank's security guard, who would get them into the bank without tripping alarms. What Roybal didn't know was that he alone would be blamed for the robbery. Small matter, that. A strong back with a weak mind—a patsy.

There were others, of course, the construction company he'd recently hired to repair the leak in Nova Bank's dramatic roof and an art restoration company lined up to "restore" the mobile.

And by now, everyone in the neighborhood was used to seeing the Planties and Bloomers truck in front of the bank, and Roybal admitted the plant-tender without so much as making him sign in. The landscaper was a little nebbish of a man who tended to the tightly trimmed topiaries that flanked the bank's front doors, and its noble palms in the corners of the lobby. He had access to every room that contained a plant of any size, from the vast marble lobby to the executive offices and lavatories.

Dawson thought of himself as a businessman—a good middleman. This whole thing was a massive pain in his backside to coordinate, and kept him busier than a one-legged man in a butt-kicking contest, what with his Congressional duties and a mistress, but the payoff would be huge. His biggest deal yet. And so, like hair on a biscuit, B. Crawford Dawson hung in. He smiled to himself, satisfied at how things were coming together.

Chapter Seventeen

The following morning Wynn read Bishop's text while she waited in traffic:

W. de la Terre

She laughed out loud at that. He'd crafted a message specifically for her dyslexic brain, and she'd unscrambled it the second she glanced at it—an anagram for Walter Reed. The National Military Medical Center. In Bethesda, Maryland. Bishop was back. Fewer than ten miles away. Less than an hour. Taking a deep breath, she relaxed and looked out her driver's side window at the sky. It was going to be a beautiful day.

Job one, when she reached her desk, was to contact the insurance company that covered the sculpture. She'd never heard of the firm, Headware Insurance. When she'd pressed Summers for the name, he'd assured her that it wasn't a hoax but a boutique insurer of costly items and important art.

Still, alarm bells went off in her head when a male voice at the Headware phone number answered with only, "Hello?"

Explaining who she was and what she wanted, she asked to be connected with the claims department.

There was a long pause. "I'm not sure I can do that."

"Do you wish to call the FBI and check my credentials?"

"Ms. Cabot, we are a small firm. We don't have a claims department per se. We all wear a lot of hats."

"Then what can you tell me, Mr.…."

"Anton Headley. My partner and I don't comment on pending claims. To anyone."

"You did know the piece was stolen?"

"We're waiting to hear on that."

"Waiting? For what?"

"Why, Ms. Cabot, for your own report. Even then, we will need to assess its veracity."

She bit back the indignation. "You don't believe the FBI's report will be accurate?"

"We have to compare it with what we know."

"If you know something that has bearing on this case—"

"I can't comment."

"I can bring you in for questioning."

"I'll check with my partner and get back to you."

* * *

Wynn Cabot pulled the Slow Pocus into a long dirt alleyway that dead-ended at a large, single-story metal building—the workshop of noted sculptor Lowell Chrysler. She circled around and backed the car up to the building, cut the engine and sighed. She'd chased so many dead-ends recently—and this one was literal—maybe this was a metaphor for things looking up.

No cars other than hers sat in front of the building, but she spotted a door on one corner of the shop, propped open with a large box fan. Voices and a brassy pounding resonated off the corrugated metal walls. She got out of her car and paused, wondering what Lowell Chrysler's role in all of this might be.

Her last case involving an artist—landscape painter Frederick MacKenzie in Napa, a man who'd hoped to fleece a family out of their vineyard estate—had ended with MacKenzie being exposed as a fraud. *Surely*, she thought, *surely, not all artists were con men, were they?*

Still, caution needed to be her watchword when approaching nameless metal buildings. She unsnapped the strap on her holster before she stepped over the box fan and into the doorway of what seemed to be a reception area of the workshop.

"G'morning," she called out and pulled out her credentials. "Folks? Anyone here?"

Conversation behind the wall stopped.

"Hello?" she said.

A man in a grimy t-shirt and cargo shorts appeared around a corner. "Oh, hi—we thought we heard someone out here."

"Right," Wynn held out a business card. "I'm Wynn Cabot."

"Andy Cardenas, Mr. Chrysler's head apprentice," he said. He studied the card for a moment and gave a low whistle. "Wowza. FBI Art Crimes. Well, lady, you've come to the right place—what we do here *is* a crime." He chuckled at his own joke. "Come in, the guys are going to want to meet you."

"I didn't see any cars…"

"We don't park out front—that's an invitation to getting your ride stripped. We built a chain-link cage for parking."

"Should I worry…" Wynn indicated her car with government plates.

Cardenas cocked his head to look out the window at her car, chuckled again and shook his head. "No ma'am, I don't think you need to worry. C'mon back."

Behind the wall, the shop opened out into one room that contained several bays for cutting, welding, painting, and crating Lowell Chrysler's mobiles. Two other men huddled over a wire armature, one in a welder's apron, the other in a white smock.

"I'm here about the Lowell Chrysler piece," Wynn said. "The one that hangs—hung—at Nova Bank. You may have heard, I don't know…it was stolen."

The man in a welder's apron frowned. "Stolen? How could that happen? It was forty feet in the air. And up there to stay—I helped install that piece."

"So did I," Cardenas said. "What happened?"

Wynn began to relax—these guys weren't a menace, and they might have information she needed. "The roof leaked and needed to be fixed. Before that could happen, the mobile needed to be moved. A bunch called Versailles Art Transport took the piece down and carried it off. Any of you ever heard of them?"

Cardenas shook his head. "I know all the outfits that do that kind of thing—Versaille's not one of them."

"No," Wynn said, "I expect not. I think they're a fake. And I think Mr. Chrysler's *Cornucopia* is gone." She thought for a moment. "How long since Mr. Chrysler has been in?"

Cardenas shrugged. "Six, seven months maybe. We're slowly chewing through his backlog of commissions. Mr. Chrysler's agent is still selling his work, even though Chrysler's not, um, he's...well, retired, I guess you could say."

"Know where I can get hold of Mr. Chrysler?"

Cardenas shook his head. "Nope, but his agent should." He stepped to a desk, pulled out a business card and handed it to Wynn. "Here. She's in Georgetown."

"Thanks." Wynn paused and looked around, then turned to the man in the painter's smock. "Did you work on *Cornucopia*?"

"That was before I came. The guy who worked on that one isn't here anymore."

Cardenas walked her to the front office and looked again at Wynn's business card. "There used to be a swimmer named Wynn Cabot—you any relation?"

Wynn smiled and hopped over the box fan in the doorway. "So I've heard. She's someone else, I think."

* * *

Art and Texture Gallery, at the corner of Wisconsin and Reservoir Road, in D.C.'s toney Georgetown, was a one-story affair with royal blue awnings. Wynn had called ahead, to be sure Beverly Browne, Lowell Chrysler's agent, would be in.

She parked in front, opened the gallery's front door and gasped. Seldom had she seen a fine art gallery with art this fine—superb paintings and sculpture presented as if in a museum, curated by period and style.

An attractive brunette approached from the back, her teal sheath dress outlining her figure. She smiled and held out her right hand. "Beverly Browne. Thank you for calling ahead—I was just about to leave for the day. And, of course, Andy Cardenas had called to say you'd been to the workshop. He was very impressed with you—and of course, I recognize you too from, well, from the Olympics, Ms. Cabot."

Wynn flashed her credentials and shook hands. "A pleasure. The gallery is quite good."

"Thank you—I'm very proud of it. We have a clientele with a sophisticated palate. My challenge is to provide them with work that's above their expectations."

"I'm here about Lowell Chrysler's work, as you know. Were you aware that *Cornucopia* has...let's say, gone missing from Nova Bank?"

Beverly Browne's reaction told Wynn part of what she wanted to know. The agent was truly startled to hear the news. "What? No. How long ago was this? I—well." The agent pushed an errant lock of dark hair out of her face, and held it with one hand, placing the other hand on her hip while she thought. "You've talked to the boys at the studio, were they of any help?"

Wynn pulled out her notepad. "How old was the mobile?"

"Let me check—it's been four years, maybe five, since it was commissioned." She turned and walked to a desk nearby, flipped through a card index and pulled out one card. "Yes, I received the check in May, four years ago."

"And who commissioned it?"

"A lovely man named Mark Bowles, that I remember. On behalf of the Jacobs family. But the check was drawn on the bank's business account, for insurance purposes."

"Andy Cardenas said you're still providing them with commissioned work for Mr. Chrysler, even though he's retired?"

Beverly Browne smiled. "Retired is a charming way of putting it. I'm sure Andy was protecting Lowell's reputation, and the reputation of the work. Andy is such a nice guy—but he knows."

"Knows?"

"Lowell Chrysler hasn't worked for—it was just before *Cornucopia* was commissioned that he began to...slip away from us. I've been selling his work from sketches…whenever I could sell it at all."

"Slip away." Wynn knew she was parroting Beverly Browne's words, but the technique was working, so she went with it.

"Early onset Alzheimer's. Lowell was only fifty-six when he was first diagnosed. He sat down and sketched like mad for about a year until he couldn't remember why he was sitting at his drawing table. The disease progressed rapidly from there. Just before Summers commissioned *Cornucopia*, Lowell's physician prescribed a new wonder drug—or it was at the time—and during that last lucid period he arranged to have himself put in assisted living. A place called Wood Creek, out in Woodbridge, Virginia."

"Did he ever marry?"

"Good Lord, no. Lowell Chrysler was barely tolerable to most people—that's why he needed an agent. I'm surprised Andy Cardenas lasted through all the verbal abuse Lowell heaped on him. But, as I say, Andy is a really sweet guy."

"Have you visited Chrysler since he's been at Wood Creek?"

"When he first moved out there, yes." Beverly Browne shook her head. "Now it wouldn't do much good. He doesn't recognize anyone. Nor does he make much sense when he speaks."

"I'm sure you can appreciate that I have to go out there anyway."

"I do. I'm sorry you have to make the trip, but I get it."

Wynn nodded. "Do you know anything about gold and silver, something that might have had to do with the sculpture?"

The agent shook her head. "The elements in *Cornucopia* were solid gold and silver on platinum rods. That's as close as I can come to gold and silver anything. Sorry."

Wynn flipped her notepad closed and checked the time on her phone—just after three o'clock.

Lowell Chrysler would keep until tomorrow. Afternoon traffic would make a visit to Wood Creek nearly impossible, and she had another stop to make before quitting time—north on Wisconsin Avenue to Bethesda.

Chapter Eighteen

Seeing Bishop this way was tougher than she'd thought it would be. He was beyond pale, his skin white almost to the point of translucent. The only color in his face was deep purple circles under his eyes.

His eyelids flickered and opened. "Hi." Grimacing, he tried to sit up.

Wynn smiled. "You have a bad case of bed head."

He flopped back onto the pillow. "If that's my biggest problem, I'm a lucky man."

"From what I understand, you're a lucky man anyway." She reached for his hand and gave it a little squeeze, holding it just a second longer than she should have.

"You shouldn't be here," he wheezed.

"How could I not be, when you told me where you were?"

"I wanted you to know I was back stateside, and safe." He took his hand away. "That's all."

His comment stung, but she chalked it up to his condition. She dragged a chair up next to the bed and dropped into it. "Well, I need your help."

"I'm not exactly in any shape…"

"I'm getting nowhere on a case and I need your advice."

For the next twenty minutes, she outlined the Nova Bank theft and her efforts so far. Wrapping up her report, she added, "So far, it's simply missing. We haven't heard of any attempts to fence it or pawn it, and there haven't been any ransom notes. It's just gone. Why would anybody take it?"

"There are a million reasons why anybody takes anything." He shifted in the bed and counted on his fingers. "To humiliate the owner. To get revenge.

Because they want the object and can't have it any other way." He gave her a thumbs up. "This one? I bet they're melting it down for the precious metals."

"That could be done anywhere—someone's garage or basement."

"You might catch the guys who took it. But my guess is, we'll never see the sculpture again."

Wynn opened her mouth to reply, but what she saw made her stop.

Linda Grazer stood inside the doorway, looking from Wynn to Bishop and back. "You know, Cabot," she said, "I shouldn't be surprised you're here, but I really am. I never guessed you'd disobey me."

"I...I...wanted—"

Bishop held up a hand. "She didn't."

Grazer set her hands on her hips. "Bishop, I'll excuse you because you're impaired. But Cabot, I told you to let it go. And you didn't. So now it's a direct order—think about whether you want to continue to work in this department. Because here's the deal—I need people to do what I tell them."

For Wynn, the dressing down felt familiar, as though she stepped through the same mental door she'd walked through when people told her she couldn't do something because of her dyslexia, or that she'd never amount to much as a swimmer. Or that she'd failed as a wife.

"You don't want people who take initiative, then," Wynn said. It wasn't a question.

"I beg your pardon?" Grazer looked confused.

"Special Agent Bishop is not just my boss, he is my partner. If he is wounded, I will do whatever I can to determine his whereabouts and ensure his safe return." She picked up her handbag, ducked around Grazer, and pointed at Bishop. "And André, I'll see *you* tomorrow."

When Wynn had gone, Grazer rounded on Bishop. "How did she know where to find you?"

He gaped at her, not making a sound.

"How did she know where you were?" Grazer's volume rose. "Because here's the deal. If she's the reason anything else goes wrong after that screw up in Jerusalem, she won't be the only one cleaning out her desk. You read me?"

He shut his mouth and then spoke. "Anything new on the case?"

"I have an idea," Grazer said. "You don't worry about what you were working on until you're able to pick it up and run with it again."

"I'm fine," he grunted.

"Get your medical and psych clearance, and you can get back to the case. Meanwhile, we'll chat about the weather, or the dress code for the cafeteria." She pivoted. "I'll keep tabs on you."

Bishop watched her storm out of the room and then made his hands into fists and pounded the bed. Damn Wynn, damn her for caring, and damn himself for giving in to her.

He recalled a moment that happened shortly after he met her. She saw that his nose was bleeding—the product of his allergies and the dry mountain air of Santa Fe—and she'd handed him a tissue. A caring gesture, even though she herself was in the throes of a mess so big it could be seen from space: her lover murdered, her callous husband the chief suspect, and a crooked sheriff more concerned with his cufflinks than with collaring the real killer.

Sent to New Mexico to investigate an art theft, Bishop learned a lot about her: the physical athleticism that saved her life, her way of moving that reminded him of silk, the dyslexia that got worse when she was tired or stressed. And her mental strengths too: a self-discipline that had made her an Olympic swimmer, her ability to spot a piece of bogus art from across a room, the way she didn't see her dyslexia as a handicap but as a difference she used to her advantage in solving art crime.

Thinking he could use that at the FBI, he'd invited her back to Washington to join the bureau the minute a spot opened up.

Now, more than a year later, he needed—what from her?

Certainly he felt stronger physically. The Israeli surgeons had done amazing work, and stateside he'd gained agility, his ribs were knitting, and he could breathe more deeply—better oxygenation, the doctors said. The wound was healing; under the bandages, a scar grew at the edges.

He didn't need someone watching over him, guarding him.

But he didn't need distance from her, either. What he needed was to get back to himself without the distraction of her. He needed, as Grazer had bluntly pointed out, to get back to work. His job wasn't only what he did for a living, it was who he was.

And he didn't want to think about where he'd be without it.

He pictured Wynn's face, her green eyes, her mop of russet curls, her look of concern when she'd handed him the tissue in Santa Fe.

He wanted…No. He shook his head.

He had to take care of himself first.

Chapter Nineteen

On Thursday, July second, after coffee and a quick review of the file at her desk, Wynn walked down the hallway at FBI Headquarters, her head down, checking her bag for her badge, keys and phone. Linda Grazer, headed the other way, stepped into Wynn's path and snapped, "Cabot!"

Wynn jerked to a halt, looking up. "Yes, ma'am?"

Grazer folded her arms. "Since you're headed for the elevator, I assume you're on your way to check out a lead." She tapped her temple. "I also have keen investigative powers."

"Yes, ma'am." Wynn stood her ground. "On all counts."

"Then tell me, what have you got and where are you going?"

"Well, the other day I was canvassing the Nova Bank neighborhood—getting totally nowhere. Nobody saw anything, nothing out of the ordinary. So I figured, follow the ordinary. I stopped into the Capitol Café—and it's a sandwich place in one of the office buildings—"

"I know it, odd as that sounds. Go on."

"—and I saw a bike courier. He said he'd been making deliveries in that area, the day the sculpture went missing."

"Deliveries to the bank?"

"Not to the bank. Couriers don't do a lot of document deliveries anymore. They started delivering flowers as a side hustle, and it's their main gig now."

"But not to the bank, not that day."

"No. But he was almost hit by a truck when he dodged a street repair crew."

"So find that crew."

"Already did. On Duddington Place and wow, is that tough to get to with all the one-way streets."

"Does this train of thought have a caboose, Cabot?"

"They were outside Nova Bank on the day, and didn't see anything. But here's—" Wynn checked herself. "Seems as how, District DOT puts up 'No Parking' signs when they're going to do repairs. And that day, in spite of the signs, someone parked there."

"Who?"

"An armored truck."

Chapter Twenty

"Step away from the truck!"

Wynn froze and extended her arms out from her sides, backed slowly away from the driver's side door of the armored truck and then turned around.

She'd caught up with the armored truck in the Starbucks parking lot at M and New Jersey, between the Navy Yard and the baseball stadium. By the time she got there, the driver, a young woman, had stayed with the truck while her partner went inside to order.

Now her partner was back, barking orders at her, one hand on the butt of his holstered gun, the other holding a cardboard tray of two coffees.

"FBI," she said. "Wynn Cabot." She pointed down at the badge that hung on a lanyard around her neck.

He crossed the little lot and eyed her badge. "You ought to know better than to walk up to our truck like that."

"Your office was supposed to tell you I was coming."

"Yeah, well, they didn't."

"Um, Rick," the driver said, "yeah, they did. They called while you were inside."

"Still," her partner said, "you could have been more careful."

Wynn watched as he handed the tray of coffees to his driver. "Friday, the nineteenth, you serviced the ATM outside Nova Bank on E. You remember that?"

"Sure do. Pain in the butt. The bank was shut for the day and the ATM ran out of cash. Somebody got upset and pounded on the keypad."

"Did you see a white sprinter van at the bank that day?" She looked from one to the other of the guards.

Their faces read blank.

The guy shrugged. "If we did, we didn't think it was a threat."

"Maybe a bike courier?"

"Don't recall one. Damn nuisances anyway."

"So you didn't see anything unusual? Out of the ordinary?"

"We don't have a lot of time for sightseeing."

"Thanks anyway." She flipped her notebook closed, climbed into the sauna that was the Slow Pocus, and headed for Woodbridge, Virginia. Time to see what Lowell Chrysler would have to say, garbled as it might be.

Mid-morning, she pulled into the driveway of Wood Creek retirement home, found a parking place, cut the engine and sighed. Visits like these always brought home her own mortality. This place looked nothing like the facility where her mother lived—this one a staid, three-story red brick affair with white columns, because this was the D.C. suburbs, while her mom's place, in Lubbock, Texas, was a series of chirpy yellow frame bungalows.

On the phone, the woman at Wood Creek had suggested Wynn come mid-morning for several reasons: Chrysler was more likely to be lucid, the traffic out to Woodbridge wouldn't be as bad, and she could stay for lunch if she wanted to. On that idea she reserved judgment—lunching with a man of reputedly bad temper might not be a picnic.

Chrysler's room was fit out in typical Colonial décor, and Chrysler sat in a wing chair near the room's lone window.

"Mr. Chrysler," Wynn said, and held out her right hand, "I'm Wynn Cabot, from the FBI. I think they told you I was coming?"

Chrysler stared down at his hands in his lap. "So?"

"I wonder if you have a moment to talk?"

"Where else would I be going? You want to talk, talk. Women are always talking. Blah blah blah."

"Do you remember fabricating your mobile called *Cornucopia*? The one with gold and silver elements?"

"Objects."

"Sir?"

"They're objects, not elements. 'Elements' sounds ridiculous. Pretentious."

"Okay, then. Objects. Gold and silver objects."

"No, I don't remember. You don't know what you're talking about, always babbling. Blah blah blah."

"I brought a photo…" Wynn held out one of the photos Summers had given her.

"Why are you asking me about this?" Chrysler began to hike up his hospital gown. "Get me a bedpan."

Wynn stepped to the door and looked both ways in the hall. No one.

"Get me a bedpan, nurse."

"I'm trying, Mr. Chrysler, but I'm not a—" She walked four paces down the hall and called, "I need a nurse."

"Blah blah blah," Chrysler yelled after her. "Go on, get me a bedpan. And then get lost."

Chapter Twenty-One

Mark Bowles' new office at FinCEN overlooked a vast parking lot, and beyond that, the Tyson's Corner shopping complex. Not the view he'd had in mind when he imagined himself another rung up in banking hierarchy, but a private office in the Special Measures division of FinCEN was apparently a privilege, so he was grateful for whatever privacy his office afforded.

The view, or lack of it, forced him to focus on the complex web of withdrawals from Nova Bank over the past six years, and deposits in foreign accounts from the Bahamas and Caymans to Switzerland and Singapore. So far, the map traced somewhere between thirty-five and forty million dollars of Nova's assets.

Bowles's Suspicious Activity Reports had detailed only a third of that; the rest had come from the foreign depositories themselves, thanks to intervention from the head of the Senate Finance Committee, Senator Jake Osborne.

After Osborne made a few overseas phone calls, faxes and elaborate emails with PDF files attached had poured forth, and now Bowles had a mess on his hands. His job was to dismantle how the bank had scammed wealthy depositors out of that much cash without their knowledge. Hundreds of times, Nova's President, Peter Summers, had withdrawn amounts just under a limit that would trigger a report known as the Currency Transaction Report, and moved the money to one of the off-shore accounts listed.

Each time the money was taken from an account deemed dormant—an account that had seen no account activity in six months—so that Summers could be reasonably sure the account holder wasn't watching his or her balance.

In the past year, though, all that money and more had been transferred back into a Nova bank account held in an alias name and then evaporated in cash, again withdrawn just under CTR limits.

Bowles sighed. Offshore banking wasn't illegal. Withdrawing money from depositors without their knowledge was. Not reporting offshore accounts was. What was Summers up to? Clearly fraud, possibly money laundering. What this required was the IRS's Criminal Investigations people, or the FBI's SWAT team of forensic accountants. The brass at FinCEN might not like it, but it was time to get those agencies involved.

Chapter Twenty-Two

On the muggy morning of Friday, July third, the tumblers to both the locks on the front door and the locks on the safe deposit vault dropped as they would on any other Friday morning. Although it was a holiday, the bank's security system treated the day and time as a normal weekday. No additional measure had been taken to override the programming that governed the system.

James Roybal badged himself into the bank building shortly before nine a.m., punched his code into the keypad and sat down in front of a row of closed circuit television cameras, all of which were aimed at empty teller stations. He sighed, envying the tellers able to sleep in on this hot, humid morning. He dialed down the air conditioning to seventy degrees.

Marlene Reese arrived moments later. Roybal rose and gave her tote a cursory once-through.

"Morning," Marlene said. "Nothing much to see in there today, James. Not even a sandwich if we're to be out of here before lunchtime."

Roybal nodded and handed over her canvas bag. "See you later, Marlene."

The Planties and Bloomers panel truck pulled up, and their lone employee got out, pruning shears in hand, to tidy the topiaries on either side of the bank's front doors. A Phelps Construction truck pulled in at the curb and discharged a passenger. Roybal flipped the latch on the double front doors and admitted Narville Phelps.

Phelps looked up at the ceiling, then turned to Roybal and shook his head. "Whoo-ee. Makes me sick to my stomach just thinking of being up there."

Roybal chuckled, "Guess you'll never be a second-story man, eh?"

"Hell, it's all I can do to be a first-story man. I live in a garden apartment for a reason. Speaking of underground, you ready?"

Phelps and Roybal walked to the bank of elevators, and Roybal held his badge to the card reader. Phelps sighed. "I don't have much taste for this, you know."

"It's for the good of the country, Dawson says."

"Can't figure out how, but I'll do it."

Roybal shook his head. "The why escapes me, too. But if a congressman…"

"You'd think, wouldn't you?"

"He knows what he's talking about, doesn't he?"

The elevator doors closed and Roybal returned to his closed circuit TV screens. He checked his watch and pulled out his phone. That new teller. Maybe she'd like to go with him to the fireworks tomorrow night. She was obviously into fitness—she had a tight little body and a nice butt. And a great name—Vivian May.

Marlene Reese looked up from her romance novel and raised a finger in Phelps' direction. She rose, unlocked the gated door that separated her desk from the vault, and returned to her book. Phelps picked up Marlene's tote bag, shifted it to the hand that held his duffle, and then tugged the huge vault door over until it nearly closed.

"Careful," Marlene said without looking up. "Can't help you if you shut yourself in."

He withdrew a list of nine safety deposit boxes, drilled and hammered out the locks on them in the space of twenty minutes, and looted their contents no matter what they were. In some cases he didn't care what the boxes contained—a small spiral-bound notebook with what looked like computer passwords in it, a bag of white powder that felt, in a taste test, like cocaine, a clutch of fake IDs. Other items bothered him more: a kid's drawings, some old scrolls that were probably worth something. Four of the boxes were, oddly enough, empty. It puzzled Phelps, but only for a moment.

He unzipped the false bottom in his canvas duffle, laid the items in and then took Marlene's tote bag and did the same. In the last of the boxes he hit pay dirt: a black canvas bag full of money and a Beretta 9mm pistol. He stashed these in one end of his duffle and set the bags outside the vault.

He took down a fire extinguisher from the wall near Marlene's desk. "Stand back," he said, and pulled a painter's respirator out of his shirt pocket.

Marlene eyed the bags and knelt. "Go do what you're supposed to do."

Phelps stepped back into the vault and began to spray fire retardant over the surface of the safe deposit boxes, the floor, and finally the gate.

While he sprayed Marlene rummaged through the items Phelps had put into his duffle and withdrew the one she sought. Sheaves from an ancient sheepskin Torah scroll. She already had its companion codex, a book she'd taken two weeks ago from the rabbi's safe deposit box. The two would once again be united, as they had been before they were stolen in the Palestinian city of Nablus in 1995. Now they were going home.

* * *

Phelps checked the time on his phone—start to finish the heist had taken an hour. He'd be out of the bank before 10:30. Marlene locked the cage door, closed the three-foot-thick solid-steel vault, rolled the tumbler handle, and dialed in her code. She and Phelps rode up in the elevator together and waved breezily to Roybal as they left by the front door.

Roybal, still on the phone with Vivian May, waved back, not bothering to check the duffle bag and tote. His duty as a front-line guardian of democracy was done.

Marlene Reese and Narville Phelps opened the back of the Planties and Bloomers panel van and threw their bags atop vestiges of peat and manure. The two of them climbed into the van and, Phelps at the wheel, headed for Marlene's small apartment on 13th Street Northwest, where Congressman B. Crawford Dawson waited.

Chapter Twenty-Three

On Monday morning Marlene left her tiny apartment and walked a block to the U Street Metro Station. She almost always found a seat on the train, or someone gave her theirs, and other passengers didn't bother the gray-haired lady with the pleasant smile.

At L'Enfant Plaza, she changed to the Blue Line and rode to the Capitol South Metro station, and then walked three blocks to the bank. This was her exercise, she told herself, her only cardio workout these days, and she moved briskly to be at the bank just before business hours began for the day. She'd never been late, not once since she'd started there, shortly after her roommate, Sandy, had died.

Ten years ago this month, she thought. Ten years of this, a new, strange life carved by others as much as by Marlene herself, ten years of watching, waiting, striving to stay upbeat, counting her blessings, such as they were, every day.

At two minutes before nine o'clock, James Roybal opened the door of Nova Bank and Marlene entered along with a blast of hot, humid air scented by car exhaust from the freeways that loomed in back of the bank, and the faint smell of the river a few blocks away, beyond the Navy Yard.

Roybal looked her in the eye for a brief moment and then bent to the usual poke through her tote bag.

Collecting her bag, she crossed the floor, stopping only briefly to look up at where the Lowell Chrysler mobile had been, a soft sigh escaping her lips before she continued on to the elevator. Although she was the only one in the car, she turned to face the door, puffing her cheeks out and wagging her head to loosen the kinks in her neck.

Below, at the vault level, she withdrew her keys to unlock her desk, booted her computer and turned on the monitor. Then she went to the vault, tapped in her code, spun the wheel that drew back the bolts, and opened the door. Balanced as it was, it still took most of her strength, and she struggled to pull it open.

And then she saw the wreckage.

It wasn't like she hadn't expected to find something amiss, but she hadn't thought the vault would be such a mess. Phelps had really overdone it with the fire extinguisher.

She reached out to touch the gate, then pulled her hand back, remembering Phelps' admonition—that the fire retardant he sprayed was to destroy any fingerprints that might be in the vault—his, hers or anyone else's. Shrugging, she walked back to her desk and picked up the phone.

"James, would you meet me at the elevator, please?"

In the lift, on the way up, she worked herself into a panic: "Oh, oh, oh, oh, oh," she moaned in increasing volume. Moving to the rear of the car, she readied herself and when the door opened, she said quietly, "James—where's Mr. Summers? We've been robbed."

Roybal feigned surprise. "What? Ms. Reese, *what?*"

Marlene wailed and dashed toward the executive quarters and Summers' office.

Empty.

She found Summers in the store room that also served as a break room, coffee in hand, about to take a bite out of a donut topped in red, white and blue sprinkles.

"Mr. Summers," she said in a gulp, "we've been robbed. We—we've been..."

Summers' grip tightened on the paper coffee cup, which collapsed and fell from his hand onto a case of copy paper. "Dammit, Marlene," he said, shaking hot coffee from his hand. "No, we haven't been robbed. The sculpture was removed so the roof could be fixed. Surely you saw the workers that day." He bit into the donut which exploded sprinkles into the spilled coffee.

Marlene tried not to watch the coffee seep into the reams of paper and spread onto the floor. "No, sir," she said, making her voice rise appropriately. "It's the vault—the safe deposit boxes. The whole thing's a mess. I think we've been robbed."

"What? For God's sake, Marlene, keep your voice down, before the customers hear you. What the hell are you talking about?"

"The vault," she rasped. "I opened the vault just now, and the boxes—we've been robbed!" Putting her hands over her eyes, she almost convinced herself that she was hysterical.

Roybal edged into the room and Summers turned to him. "Can you calm her down? I don't want the customers to hear any of this. Maybe we all better go back down to the vault and see what's going on."

* * *

When faced with a crisis, Howard Jacobs had a three-step method for handling the offender: First, remind them that they were somehow beholden to him for some favor, real or imagined.

Second, if the first ploy didn't work or didn't apply, yell at them and, if necessary, yell louder. Use profanity and offensive language to unnerve them.

And third, if the first one doesn't work, and the offender isn't fazed by guilt or the f-bomb, threaten them. For individuals, threaten to cancel their bonuses, threaten to bust them to a lower pay grade, threaten to fire them. For companies, threats of revoking their contracts, going to the competition or ruining them financially were usually sufficient.

His meltdown had come when he learned of the robbery. Peter Summers, overloaded on caffeine and sugar by 10:30 Monday morning, had reached the last name on the list: Howard Jacobs. Not knowing how to put it off any longer, he'd dialed Jacobs at home and told him the news.

"Well, there's been, ah, an irregularity in the safe deposit boxes."

Jacobs snapped. "Irregularity? What the hell are you talking about?"

"It appears some of the boxes were tampered with."

"Summers, I put you in that position because I trusted you. And now—"

"It must've happened over the weekend. The boxes were opened, and the contents...taken."

"All of the boxes?" Jacobs felt his jaw start to clench and beads of sweat broke out on his forehead.

"No, no. Let me count. Nine. Nine boxes."

Jacobs felt his blood pressure ratchet up. His voice began in a low growl and rose in both pitch and volume as he said, "For the love of all that is holy, Summers, tell me that my box was not one of them."

Summers let out a long, slow breath. "Actually, Howard—"

All Summers could hear was a banging noise as Jacobs beat his phone against a wall. Then expletives came, rapid fire, and some insinuations that Summers couldn't locate his backside with a GPS and a heat-sensing camera.

"Summers!" Jacobs finally said. "You listen to me and you listen good. I will be there within the hour and we will decide what to do. And have your VP of PR standing by."

Summers gulped. "Mr. Bowles resigned a few days ago."

"Who took his place?"

Summers didn't reply.

"You've hired somebody, haven't you?"

Summers looked out his window and pursed his lips. "We're still reviewing resumes."

*Howard Jacobs couldn't find anyone to blame immediately for the nightmare that faced Nova Bank. He and Summers looked at the vault, gleaming after its thorough cleaning. James Roybal had called in the janitorial service to mop up, and the fresh lemon scent of the sparkling tableau in the vault belied the fact that they'd been robbed.

Summers tried to placate Jacobs as they assessed the damage to the boxes. "We'll have these repaired in no time, Howard. Good as new, by the first of August."

Jacobs leaned over to touch the open door of his own safe deposit box. He swore again and slammed the door, only to have it spring open again. His eyes fell on Marlene Reese. She kept her face impassive as she watched Jacobs spit and spew.

Jacobs paced. "You're sure we're not responsible?"

"No, Howard, no for the third time," Summers said. "Nova Bank is not liable in any way. It's one thing I am sure of."

As he lifted his feet into bed on Monday night, Howard Jacobs recalled a time when, in the third grade, he'd thrown a lit cherry bomb down a toilet at school; the explosion had resulted in water and waste raining down over the boys' restroom, and a world of hurt landing on Howard Jacobs' eight-year-old head.

He felt the same way now. Things had gone straight down the crapper at the bank today and then exploded upwards. Yes, he and Summers knew that box holders who were affected would call their insurance companies.

The insurance companies would, in turn, contact MPD, who would swear they had no knowledge of a problem at Nova Bank, other than a missing sculpture. Some of the insurers would be, understandably, reluctant to pay claims based on hearsay, but two box holders and their agents weren't about to be ignored.

One was a golfing buddy of Jacobs' insurance agent, and another's agent was related to Sherryl Jacobs' sister. Throughout the afternoon they hung on like terriers, keeping up a steady stream of phone calls until, late in the day, Summers had been forced to call MPD and admit to a break-in.

As Jacobs watched, Summers spoke to officer Frosty Winters, tossing off the event lightly, almost like a joke: "We had a bit of a pesky problem."

Then Winters sent two officers to look at the now-cleaned-up scene of the crime, where they'd found nothing, save for nine drilled safe deposit box doors. The police took photos, dusted for prints, made notes and left without comment.

Jacobs and Summers had thought they were off the hook, never dreaming Winters would turn over the safe deposit box heist to the FBI.

Just before the bank closed, the FBI's Bank Theft division paid Nova a personal visit—since they were close—and gave Summers and Jacobs a stern lecture on the need to report crimes of any kind immediately. They demanded the list of customers whose boxes had been drilled.

Good God, Jacobs thought, the FBI. This was getting out of control. How was he ever going to rein it in? All the law enforcement traffic at Nova today wasn't exactly a hallmark of bank stability.

Jacobs' wife, Sherryl, padded barefoot across the spacious master bedroom from the sitting area. "Are you okay, baby?"

"Hard day at the bank." He pulled a sheet over himself and turned away from her.

Dropping her satin wrap, she slid under the cover and snuggled up behind him. "Can I do anything to help?"

"No." He left no doubt. "Not tonight."

She pulled back to her side of the bed. "You'll get it straightened out in the morning, tiger."

Jacobs grunted, turned out his bedside lamp, and stared into the darkness.

His greatest worry right now was the recovery of that Torah scroll—the fabled Abisha scroll supposedly written in the 14th century. That damned thing had a habit of going missing—it had been stolen from its ark in the Palestinian city of Nablus in 1995 along with its 15th century codex, but no one in Nablus wanted to talk about who might've done the robbery. Next anyone saw the scroll, it had gone from Palestine to Jordan to England and vanished again until a few weeks ago when Jacobs had arranged for its purchase from a black marketeer in Jerusalem.

He'd given it, with due flourish, to his rabbi, who, in turn had appointed him to his synagogue's Board of Trustees—a position that not only put Jacobs at the top of the synagogue's pecking order, but gave him access to Washington's movers, shakers and money-makers. All he had to do was keep his ears open and he could get in on the most lucrative real estate deals, investments and shakedowns in town.

The rabbi had asked Jacobs to put the Torah scroll in his own safe deposit box.

He'd risked his life for that scroll. He'd first heard it was for sale from another black market source; he imagined they all had their own underground network, and they knew he'd be in the market for the companion piece to the codex. He'd got the money together, concocted a story about a bankers' convention in Cincinnati, and took off for Jerusalem.

But when the night came for the purchase, it all went wrong. The seller wanted more money. And when Jacobs reached into his jacket, the shooting started.

Jacobs panicked—it's hard to think, let alone think coolly, when bullets are flying. He'd grabbed the Torah, run from the restaurant, and hired an unlicensed driver to take him directly to Ben Gurion Airport in Tel Aviv, where he spent four sweaty hours hoping not to be recognized by anyone in the black market network while he waited to board the first flight back to D.C.

Stateside, he got more than his reward when he presented the codex and its companion Torah to the rabbi. The old man heaped praise on Jacobs, assuring him that his place in the World to Come was rock solid, and then he handed the scroll back to Jacobs, thinking it wise to split up the Torah and the codex, instructing Jacobs to store the Torah in his own safe deposit box, even as the rabbi kept the codex in his.

Jacobs assured him that the scroll would be in a vault as secure as Fort Knox, climate controlled to a perfect seventy-two degrees and thirty percent humidity.

Now, the Torah was gone.

He threw off the sheet, sat up on the edge of the bed and gazed numbly at the home screen on his phone. He was reasonably sure his insurance policy wouldn't cover the loss of a priceless religious artifact, and he needed to get it back before the rabbi found out it was gone.

But where to start looking? Other synagogues? Rare book sellers? Antiquities dealers? Or his black market contacts—did he dare tell anyone it was missing?

Chapter Twenty-Four

I f anyone had asked Wynn how she knew that something was up, that something had shifted, she would have answered that she didn't know, not really. Sitting at her desk, she'd felt a series of undefined sensations, vibes she couldn't put a name to, that resulted in a conclusion later confirmed by someone else.

Her first inkling she chalked up to nerves. She'd been flippant—almost insubordinate—okay, insubordinate with Art Crimes Program Manager, Linda Grazer, the previous week. She'd reached the end of her tolerance for comments from Grazer, her co-workers and the people she dealt with in public—comments that showed their total lack of trust in her loyalty and in her work. She was fiercely loyal, she worked hard at her job, and wanted to do well. And she felt a sense of achievement when she reunited stolen art with its owner.

Wynn also worried about Bishop and wanted to know he was healthy, safe and home. Or at least on the mend, out of harm's way and in the general vicinity.

And that was the second cause of her jitters: a realization that she was happier to see Bishop than propriety dictated, since he was only her boss. She'd been too relieved to see him and far too sensitive when he'd rebuked her for coming to his hospital room.

Did she really care for him? It would be hard, she thought, to spend most of your days with someone and *not* care for them. Or would it? People hated their bosses all the time. Maybe familiarity did breed contempt. But when she'd worked for Seamus Caine, she'd loved him. As she would love a father, she supposed—although since her own father was absent during her childhood, she really didn't know.

This felt different.

Gio Leo was a kind man, but he lived on the opposite coast, coming to D.C. every two to three months. They talked on the phone often in the interim, but being close to someone every day, working together, solving problems, sharing the same goals—that was different, wasn't it?

Or maybe…maybe it was simply that without her ex-husband, without a steady love interest, without the basics of a relationship in her life, she was making her normal, protective feelings toward Bishop into something they weren't. Or shouldn't be.

Still, she sensed a drift in the air around her that convinced her it wasn't her own nerves that signaled something going on. She knew. An electricity that lifted her blood pressure, widened her awareness, put her on alert. A vague but rising energy, the way the decibel level goes up in a restaurant as patrons come in. A buzz around FBI Headquarters that shimmered and formed and grew until, when it was almost palpable, Wynn's phone rang and she jumped.

The caller was Grazer's assistant.

Grazer wanted to see Wynn.

Immediately.

* * *

"So here's the deal," Grazer began as Wynn sat. "I was going to ask you if you'd given any thought to what I said last week."

"As a matter—"

Grazer whipped her fingers horizontally in front of her throat, the universal "cut" gesture. "Because here's the deal. Apparently, a lot of people took off for their summer vacation this week, so the whole bureau's short-staffed. And there's been another problem at Nova Bank."

"Nova. Again?"

"Safe deposit boxes this time. Someone went in over the weekend, drilled out a bunch of boxes and took the contents. Maybe."

"Maybe? Either they did or—"

"Bank Theft Division suspects a double whammy."

The blank look on Wynn's face spoke volumes, and Grazer sighed. "A double whammy is when the box holders remove the contents from their boxes. Then thieves," Grazer held her fingers mid-air in quotes, "break in, drill the boxes and leave a mess. The box holders declare their stuff as stolen and their insurance companies pay out."

Wynn frowned in thought. "Then that means…"

"Exact-a-mundo. It's an inside job." Grazer picked up a pen. "The box holders would have to be told the theft was coming, to remove their stuff ahead of time."

"Wouldn't they know they'd be found out?"

"It's not their responsibility—safe deposit boxes aren't insured by banks—any of them. Plus, it gets worse. I've got word that FinCEN's already involved on the financial side. Sounds like Nova Bank is as porous as my will power when I'm around chocolate."

Wynn snickered at that, but Grazer didn't. She pointed her pen at Wynn. "So here's the deal, Cabot. I'm not happy with you. And as your punishment, you're assigned to the entire Nova Bank mess—missing sculpture, safe deposit heist, the whole enchilada."

Wynn's jaw dropped. "But the Bank Theft division—"

"Bank Theft gets reports north of 5,000 robberies every year. Only a tenth of those involve the vaults, but that's still better than one a day. Anyway, they brought up Nova Bank on the computer, saw we're working on the missing art, so they handed us the rest of this mess."

She tossed the pen on the desk and leaned back. "Coordinate with FinCEN and wrap it up. And Cabot?" Grazer's smile was clearly smug. "Good freakin' luck on this one."

Chapter Twenty-Five

A pink "While You Were Out" message the rabbi found on his desk when he returned from lunch read, "Safe deposit box issue, codex missing." No caller name was noted, no return phone number.

His part-time secretary had left for the day, but he knew the message wasn't in her scribble; this script was far more florid than an eighty-year-old with arthritis could manage.

He stepped to the door of his office, looking for whoever might have taken the message. No one.

He scrolled through numbers on his cell phone until he found the one he wanted and hit the green icon. By the time Howard Jacobs answered, the rabbi's blood pressure had shot up thirty points.

Finding a parking place anywhere near Nova Bank at midday was a problem, even for a vehicle as small as Wynn Cabot's elderly government-issue Focus. Inside the bank, a woman in MPD blues spoke with Roybal, the two of them chatting casually, while a man in a closely tailored navy serge suit talked to one of the tellers, an attractive young woman whose name plate proclaimed her to be Vivian May.

Wynn approached Peter Summers' office, paused at his secretary's desk, and flashed her credentials. "Here to see Mr. Summers."

The secretary gestured behind her. "So are these gentlemen."

Wynn turned, smiled at the two men and held out her ID. "Wynn Cabot, guys. I'm the FBI agent in charge of the case."

One of the men stood. "Are you now? I'm Mark Bowles, formerly of this bank. I'm with FinCEN now. We're the investigating agency here."

Wynn squared her shoulders. "Are you now?" She turned to the other man waiting to see Summers. "And you? Do you think you're the investigating agency here too?"

The man remained seated, and when he spoke to her he didn't look up. "I'd heard you'd been put in charge, Agent Cabot. I'm Frank Freund—from the FBI's Forensic Accountant Support Team. We're two floors below where your office is…"

"Wait a minute," Bowles said. "This is my case—I've been tracking this for years, filing SARs, doing the detail work. You can't take this away—"

Wynn shook her head. "I'm not here to take your case away, Mr. Bowles. I'm investigating the break-in of some safe deposit boxes, and the theft—or possible theft—of the Lowell Chrysler mobile."

Bowles' jaw dropped. "The mobile? Stolen? The safe deposit boxes?"

"Yes. Yes, to both."

"What the hell's been going on here?"

"How long ago did you leave the bank?"

"Mid-June—about three weeks ago."

Wynn nodded. "Then, just before the roof leak?"

"The day after."

Wynn glanced at Agent Frank Freund, who furiously scribbled notes as she and Bowles talked. She turned her attention back to Bowles. "Are you the man Roybal says arranged for the crew to come in to remove the mobile?"

"No. I never had the chance. Summers and I quarreled that morning, and Roybal walked me out shortly after we—rather, they—opened for business that day."

"And you conveniently end up working for FinCEN."

"They have me doing casework in their Special Measures group."

"Who's the guy in the navy suit out there talking to Vivian May?"

Bowles shrugged.

Freund looked up from his notes and shrugged back.

"He's IRS," the secretary said. "From their Criminal Investigation department."

Bowles nodded. "I was in PR here at Nova Bank. Numbers aren't my long suit—people are. I called the IRS's CI division in—they do a lot with money laundering, and I think that's part of what's going on."

"Wow. Huh. Well, we've got Frank Freund from FBI Forensics on the case, so I'll un-call them in."

Wynn was good at numbers—her dyslexia facilitated her seeing solutions to math problems in ways most folks never saw them. But she had a couple of larcenies to focus on right now, or Linda Grazer would be telling her "the deal," and it wouldn't be good news. She looked at Bowles. "Right. Let me know if I can help. Agent Freund will be your numbers guy, and I'm on the thefts, but you're point man on the finances, Bowles. That work for you?"

Mark Bowles smiled broadly. "Sure. Yeah. That makes sense." He held out his right hand to Freund, who looked up, startled. "Agent Freund, you and I have some talking to do."

Wynn turned again to the secretary. "I still need to talk to Mr. Summers."

"He's on a call."

"I'll wait, right here." She leaned against the secretary's desk where she could see the phone console. "The minute I see that light go out, I'm in there, unannounced. Okay?"

"Okay, but it's someone from Capitol Hill. It could take a while."

"I've got time," Wynn said. "Meanwhile, I'll go give that guy from the IRS the rest of the day off. Or should I give him time enough to make a date with Ms. May?"

The secretary sniffed. "Pfft. I'm sure the first thing she did was to give him her phone number. She's, well, she's like that."

* * *

Peter Summers ended his call with Congressman B. Crawford Dawson and sat back in his chair. He hadn't anticipated the legion of law enforcement that swarmed the bank that morning—someone was bound to uncover something he didn't need to have revealed. Ever. To anyone. Now he had Mark Bowles waiting outside, and his secretary had said Bowles was working for FinCEN now. Too, she'd mentioned something about the IRS nosing around, and a

Forensic Accountant from the FBI wanting access to files.

Nor had he anticipated his office door being flung open and Wynn Cabot marching in like a force of nature.

"I'm busy," Summers said.

"Yes, me too." Wynn sat opposite him and pulled out her notepad. "I have a few questions and—"

Summers rose, grabbed his coffee cup, and circled away from his desk to the bar on a console where he poured himself a short shot of bourbon. His back to her, he held up the bottle. "Miss Cabot? It's Blanton's—none better."

Wynn frowned. "Thanks, but no."

Summers set his cup down and walked up behind her, placing his hands gently on her shoulders. "Maybe you'll come back this evening then?"

"Mr. Summers, remove your hands. Now."

Summers moved his fingers up onto her neck and under her hair.

Wynn stood and turned to face him. "We can do this now, or we can do it in an interrogation room, Mr. Summers. Your choice. You keep your hands to yourself and we can talk here. You don't feel like you can control yourself, I can ask you down to headquarters—where there is no Blanton's. Or nice furniture. Or Oriental rugs."

"I have nothing to say to you in my capacity as President of this bank, Agent Wynn."

Wynn smirked. "Agent Cabot."

He opened his office door. "Doris, Agent Wynn is leaving. And don't you dare let anyone else barge in like that, ever again—there are plenty of other women who want your job."

Doris glared, first at Wynn and then at her boss. "Howard Jacobs is on line one."

For a moment, Summers watched Wynn Cabot walk out into the lobby and then he quietly shut his office door, locked it, slumped into his desk chair, downed the Blanton's in a gulp, and picked up the phone.

"Do I need this shit right now?" Jacobs began, his voice pitched an octave higher and louder than necessary. "What I don't need is to hear that the rabbi's safe deposit box has been cleaned out."

"I don't understand, Howard, where is this coming from?"

"Where it's coming from is a call I just got from my rabbi, saying he heard his safe deposit box has 'issues' too and that it's been cleaned out. So help me, Summers, if that's true, you're finished down there."

Summers sat forward, thinking. Both Dawson and Jacobs needed him right where he was—team work made the scheme work. His job was assured as long as they needed him. Fools. They were both fools if they thought they held the upper hand. "Look, I've got other shit to deal with right now—that damned FBI agent just left my office, Mark Bowles has sicced FinCEN and the IRS on us, and there's a forensic auditor waiting outside who wants to talk to me. I don't know anything about the rabbi's box, Howard, but I'll find out when I fucking get around to it."

"Like you didn't know anything about the sculpture being stolen or the thefts this weekend. I swear I am up to here with having my bank looted behind my back." Jacobs went quiet for a moment and then, "While I have you," Jacobs said, "we need more money."

"I know. I just heard from Dawson that he's gone through the last of what I'd put in the account."

"Up Dawson's credit line, then, and transfer the funds—to me this time. Dawson's spending too much on his women and the damn election. I'll deal with Dawson if he kicks about it. And Summers? Call me back about the rabbi's deposit box."

"As I said, I'll find out when I get to it. In the meantime, you and Dawson need to do something about these investigations. This has got to stop."

FBI Forensic Accountant Frank Freund piled three archive boxes of files on his kitchen table, sat down, and stared out the window to the parking lot beyond.

Never had he encountered such a bunch as he'd interviewed at Nova Bank—from airheaded teller, Vivian May, to haughty bank president Peter Summers, and wholly uncreative former employee Mark Bowles. He'd not come across a group so unqualified to run a financial institution in his many years of this work.

At least Bowles had been clever enough to spot the irregularities while he still worked for Nova—and he wasn't even privy to the worst of it. All Bowles knew was what he'd seen in lists of outgoing and incoming wire transfers that Vivian May had handled, but that was enough to file Suspicious Activity Reports with FinCEN. Fortunately, Bowles had made copies of the lists of transfers—twenty pages of them in all.

To Freund, the answer to what had been going on leaped off the page immediately, it was so clear. Money was moved from inactive accounts at Nova to offshore accounts in the Caymans, Singapore and Geneva, and then, a month later, moved back into a single account at Nova, an account that was anonymous but for a number. That account was then nearly drained each of the twenty times it was funded.

And the transfers now numbered twenty-one; the receiving account at Nova had been funded again, just yesterday.

The only person who could have access to all the pieces of the puzzle was Peter Summers himself. All of the pieces pointed to him, even the withdrawals. Yet accounts with Nova or any other bank couldn't be checked out without the account holder's permission, or a search warrant. In his talk with Summers, the arrogant bastard had made it clear he wasn't going to let the FBI take a look at the bank's accounts willingly.

Freund sighed again, turned to his computer, and opened a new PowerPoint file. Time to show the courts what he had.

He worked for the better part of the evening, glancing up occasionally when a car door slammed in the parking lot in front of his condo—fellow bureaucrats returning from work, or coming in from grocery shopping, or leaving to meet friends for dinner.

His cheery new first floor condo, close to FBI headquarters, lent itself to a goldfish-bowl existence that suited Freund. He liked watching people's daily lives unfold and then refold; there was comfort in it.

He carefully outlined, on his slides, the procedure for declaring a bank account inactive, or dormant, and what happens to the money if the account is inactive but before that cash is ultimately turned over to the District of Columbia.

And then, in his appeal for a search warrant for the numbered account, he created a chart with boxes indicating the dormant accounts with arrows that pointed to other boxes marked "LIBC Caymans," and "G&K Singapore," and "Asset Protection Associates, Geneva." At the bottom of that slide, all the arrows pointed to a box marked "Numbered Account, Nova Bank," an account that had seen more than ten million dollars come and go in eighteen months.

Freund needed to see who owned that account and how the money had been spent.

What sounded like a motorcycle pulled up, just out of sight of his kitchen window. Rather than lean to see which neighbor was coming in or going out, Freund pulled a thumb drive from his pocket, plugged it into his laptop and pulled up the proper drive.

When he heard his front door open, he opened his email file, typed in the name he intended, attached his PowerPoint file, and hit "Send," just before he felt the first blow.

Wynn picked red onions out of her gyro sandwich and set them on a tissue. She wasn't in the mood for onions; they occasionally played havoc with her stomach, and she didn't want onion breath anyway. But Grazer had ordered Greek food for the entire squad so maybe they wouldn't grouse about all the overtime, and Wynn wanted to be a team player. So she picked the onions out and ate what was basically a chicken and cucumber sandwich.

She didn't mind overtime. Her life right now consisted of long days at work, swimming for exercise on the weekends and every-other-day trips to Bethesda to visit Bishop at Walter Reed Hospital. But he'd be going home, and while visiting him in a public setting like Walter Reed was one thing, going to his place in Georgetown would be awkward and uncomfortable. Bishop was making progress; he would be released soon.

Getting the surveillance footage from the bank hadn't been the ugly scene she'd feared, but it wasn't pleasant, either.

The bank's guard, James Roybal, was civil but curt, answering her in clipped sentences instead of his former open courtesy. "Ma'am, like I said before, the cameras don't—"

"James, James," she'd said at the time, hoping the familiarity would grate on him. She shook her red curls and looked at the ceiling where the sculpture used to hang. "We can do this the easy way, where you give me the footage willingly, or I can get a court order for your entire closed circuit system and arrest you for obstruction." She stared at him with unsmiling eyes.

"There isn't anything on it for that weekend. I checked."

"I'm sure you did." Handing him a thumb drive, she'd leaned over his counter and fixed him with a stare like a retinal scan. "But I want Thursday, July second, up through and including Monday, July sixth." She'd watched his Adam's apple bob up and down at that, and then stood back while he downloaded the footage onto the drive.

When he'd finished, he'd handed it to her without a word. She took it and left, silent herself.

Now, while she'd scanned the footage from Thursday, she studied the tattoo on the back of Vivian May's left shoulder, questioning why Ms. May wasn't freezing in her sleeveless top in the sub-zero air conditioning at the bank.

The footage of Friday, July third came up on the screen, and she felt obliged to study every frame. This would be mind-numbing, she knew, since the tellers hadn't worked that day and there was really nothing to look at. Certainly no tattoos.

Clicking through the hours encapsulated in the footage, she felt her eyelids droop from boredom and carb-induced sleepiness. She watched the teller counter go from the darkness of early morning to drab as light from the rising sun crept through the windows, to full-on bright when the lobby lights came on.

Without the distraction of the tellers at their stations, though, and no customers to stand patiently at the "Please Wait Here for the Next Available Teller" sign, it was easy to see the expanse of marble floor beyond the counter.

So she dug in. And watched.

And found she could click through the frames of video much faster.

She sped up the footage so much, in fact, that she almost missed an ethereal shadow that moved across the top of her screen. A wispy gray thing that moved in rhythm, bouncing from right to left. A moving shape she thought at first was a hiccup in the video, a flaw that had occurred perhaps when Roybal transferred it, or simply dust on her computer. Or a reflection of someone walking by her desk.

She stopped the recording.

No. Yes.

It was a reflection, all right. A reflection on that pricey, polished marble floor.

And in a millisecond, Wynn's dyslexia had the reflection in the video turned right side up in her mind, and she saw an image clear and distinct: James Roybal, walking to the elevator.

With someone else.

Grazer watched the footage as Wynn re-played it in Grazer's office. "So, it's the guard?"

"It sure looks from this like he's in on it."

"Who's the other guy?"

"I can't tell. Can't see his face in the reflection, not clearly enough. But look at this." Wynn fast-forwarded the footage to show Roybal walking back across the floor by himself. "And this, too." Again she skipped forward in the footage, this time about an hour's worth. "That's our mystery man, walking back across the floor. With a woman."

"How can you tell it's a woman?"

"The shoes, the bare legs, the hemline of a skirt."

"You can tell all that? I don't see it."

"Yes, ma'am. It's a woman, all right. And there are only three women at Nova who aren't tellers. One's Summers' secretary and one's an investment advisor—and neither of them would have been at work that day. The third is the woman who's in charge of the safe deposit boxes." Wynn checked her notes. "Marlene Reese. I need to get her and Roybal in to interview them, that's for sure."

"Have at it."

Wynn swallowed hard. She hated to admit, especially to the boss, that she needed help, but this was a time to be smart. "Roybal's a big guy, and fit."

"And I'm short on personnel. You took down guys twice your size in your training at Quantico."

Wynn straightened. Grazer had obviously read her file. "And…he'll probably be armed."

Grazer wrinkled her nose; it made her eyes squint. "Here's the deal. I'll give you two guys for the afternoon. You don't bring in both the guard and the woman, I want to know why."

Chapter Twenty-Six

"Ms. Reese, you're not helping yourself here."

Sitting across a table in an interrogation room, Wynn fixed Marlene Reese with a stare, knowing that if it came down to a contest, she would win. Her Olympics training had served her well; she had faced down other champions with that look, and it calmed her breathing, lowered her heart rate and her center of gravity, and wasn't to be shaken, even today, knowing that Linda Grazer was watching on the other side of the two-way mirror on the wall to her right.

This situation was no worse than having a tough coach scrutinize her every dive, every stroke. *I've got this,* she thought. *I can outlast all of you.*

But Marlene Reese was no pushover. She gave Wynn a kindly smile and gazed squarely back. "I honestly don't know what I could tell you that would help."

Wynn decided the woman was either a pathological liar, or her personal issues ran so deep that they overrode any anxiety she might have about fabricating a story. "See, from our point of view, Marlene," she said, "it doesn't look good. We have evidence that you were involved with the thefts from the safe deposit boxes."

Marlene looked down at her hands. "I don't see how that can be."

"We have you at the scene."

Lifting her head, Marlene tilted it to one side." I wasn't there. You're mistaken."

Wynn made a show of looking at her watch. "I'm going to step out for a bit."

"Can I go home soon?"

"We're looking at that. I'll be back, and in the meantime, I want you to think about whether or not you want to change any answers. Or give us more information." Wynn was out the door before Marlene could respond.

Marlene scanned the interview room and took a deep breath. She would wait; she had no choice. But she wished she'd taken her car to work today. A wheezing Cavalier that Sandy had always called the Cadavalier, the car had been around so long it was like part of the family. Sandy had preceded it in death, so it remained Marlene's semi-trusty go-to on days when the weather was cold, or rainy, or both.

But this was high summer, and she'd taken the train that morning, which meant that when the FBI was done, they wouldn't be taking her back to her car. They'd take her to a train stop.

She didn't mind public transportation as a rule; she only avoided it at night. Not because it was dangerous, but because it reminded Marlene of the endless trips to the hospital that she'd made when Sandy was dying. Ten years ago. Parking at the hospital was at a premium back then and navigating crowded D.C. streets after dark was more than Marlene could handle safely. So, she'd taken trains and put up with the crazies and the troublemakers, and sat quietly, picturing Sandy's haggard face and praying for a better outcome for her.

She'd braved the darkened hospital sidewalks, stood on empty train platforms, waited for the two a.m. bus from Dupont Circle that took forever, but the driver talked to her to keep her awake. Within only a few weeks, Sandy was gone. Marlene was bereft.

She still hated public transportation, not for the peril of a woman traveling alone, but for the memories it brought back.

Today, maybe someone from the FBI could drive her home.

Julie "Frosty" Winters pulled on a mask, Tyvek booties, and latex gloves, though she hated gloving up in this damnably hot weather. She ducked under the crime scene tape, studied the corpse that lay at her feet, and stifled a gag—as long as she'd worked homicide, the smell of a body that had been dead for more than a couple of days still overcame her.

This one, though male, lay in the same arrangement as the female they'd found near Nova Bank last month—the body face down, legs splayed, the head twisted on the neck to face up. The same MO.

Winters reached into the right rear pants pocket of the body's khaki work pants, withdrew a wallet and flipped it open to reveal a driver's license issued in the name of Narville Phelps. Little in the way of folding money—a couple of fives and a one. A business card that read: Phelps Construction—No Job To Small.

Little else on the card except a phone number written in pencil on the back. Winters pulled out her cellphone and dialed. The call rolled immediately to a Verizon recording.

She looked around the construction site—a building being framed was still a steel skeleton, just out of the ground. Dump trucks full of fill-dirt and gravel came and went—last week's mud had turned to dust—tire marks and footprints would be impossible to find.

If a murderer wanted to hide a body, it would have been a simple matter: dump him in the excavation and throw a little debris on him. The hole was large enough that no one looked to see where the fill was being deposited. A corpse could be covered in one truck-load. Whoever did this wanted this body to be found, just as he'd left socialite Rima Arazi in Nova Bank's parking lot to be found.

Of course, Phelps might have had business with the contractor—everyone involved with the construction would be a suspect until proven otherwise. What a mess.

The only mercy in Phelps's death was that his neck was snapped so severely he'd died instantly.

Between finding the well-heeled Rima Arazi with her head snapped in the same way in June and now this guy—who owned a small construction company, but had probably never rubbed elbows with the likes of Rima Arazi in his life—these killings had begun to look like the work of a serial killer.

Wynn, meanwhile, was calculatedly irritating the crap out of James Roybal by confirming the minutiae of his dossier over and over again. Spelling of name, check. Address, phone, driver's license numbers, check. When she sensed him getting frustrated, she turned a page in her notes and started a new tack.

"Where are you from, James?"

"Santa Fe, New Mexico. Ma'am."

She nodded. "I know Santa Fe. Spent a month there one week."

"It's changed a lot."

"This was a couple of years ago. I helped bust a local sheriff."

His face registered comprehension. "Oh? That was you? I heard about that."

"Yeah. It's what got me interested in working for the FBI. You, now," she pretended to consult her notes, "you want to go work for MPD."

"Should have known you'd check."

"Other way around, actually, MPD contacted us. They always do with prospective recruits, to see if we have anything on them. When I brought up your name today, it was already flagged."

"I don't want to be a bank guard forever."

"I don't think you need to worry about that." She pushed the file to one side. "Because MPD doesn't want you if you're a felon."

"But I'm not, I haven't—"

Clenching her teeth, she drew in breath around her molars. "See, James, we know you have. That footage you gave me the other day? You're on it."

"On the Thursday footage."

Shaking her curly head, she raised her eyebrows. "On the Friday, July third, recording. The day the bank was supposed to be closed. We've got you and Marlene Reese and someone else all crisscrossing the lobby floor that day."

"No way. The date on the footage is wrong."

"It's the correct day, all right. The tellers weren't working that day."

"But the cameras don't point—"

"Yeah, they do. That marble floor that you all are so proud of, the one that's polished like a mirror? That's exactly what it is, a mirror. So that even though you're out of the frame, your reflection is right there in it."

He pounded the table but said nothing.

"Everybody said the safe deposit boxes were drilled over the holiday weekend," she said. "Now we learn they weren't."

Looking away, he pressed his lips together.

"Do you want an attorney?" she asked.

"I don't need an attorney."

"Let the record show the interviewee declined to have an attorney present." She wrote on her notes. "So you know nothing about the heist."

He exhaled out his nose, sounding like a freight train. "Look," he began. "I'll tell you what I know. No, wait. You'd never believe it." He chewed a fingernail. "Well, Marlene's probably spilled the entire story already, so I might as well. But I warn you, it'll sound crazy."

He leaned forward. "A few weeks ago, I got a visit from Congressman Dawson..."

"Do you believe him?" Grazer asked Wynn outside the interrogation room.

"Stranger things have happened."

"That story's so far-fetched, it might be true."

"If it's true..."

"We could aim for Dawson all we want and end up shooting ourselves in the foot." Grazer folded her arms. "We'll cross that bridge when we get there."

"If we get there. I'll go talk to Ms. Reese again."

Back in the interview room where Marlene sat, Wynn used the same tactic she'd used on Roybal, spending a lot of time on picky details, to Marlene's bafflement.

"You live alone?" Wynn asked.

"Yes."

"Ever been married?"

Marlene's face clouded, and Wynn knew she'd touched a nerve.

"Agent Cabot, I am gay," Marlene said. "Years ago, I met someone. But it still wasn't legal to marry."

"I see."

"Do you? I don't. What does my sexual orientation have to do with anything?"

"It doesn't. We want to determine your veracity." Wynn flipped the file closed. "Because frankly, your colleague just told us a pretty fantastic story and we want to know if one or the other of you—or both—are unbalanced or…"

"Lying."

"Your term, not mine."

Marlene glanced toward the two-way mirror and nodded. She hadn't expected James to give up so fast. Still, he had his whole life ahead of him, unlike hers. She had little to lose at this point.

On the other hand, the one person they could give up easily was the one with the non-stick coating; whatever the FBI threw at him would slide off and end up in the garbage. He was the very man against whom the FBI could do nothing—or at most, very little.

She almost felt sorry for Wynn Cabot, the earnest agent who was trying so hard, and who would be in the soup soon enough.

Marlene sighed. "Very well, then. I'll give a statement."

"Do you want an attorney present?"

"I don't think I'll need one, since I was operating at the request of the United States Government. Congressman B. Crawford Dawson asked me to participate in what he called 'a matter of national security…'"

The door to the interview room jerked open and Linda Grazer stuck her head in. "Cabot, a moment."

Wynn stepped out into the hallway. "Quickly—Marlene Reese is about to talk. What's up?"

"I just heard from MPD—you'd been looking for a guy named Phelps?"

"Yes. He's MIA."

"Nope. He's DOA—the coroner's got him. Neck broken. Clean break—a one-eighty on his body. And he's not the only one they've seen that way lately. Woman named Rima Arazi—part of a black market bunch that ran stolen artifacts out of the Middle East—was found in Nova Bank's parking lot. Coincidence? I don't think so. Find out what the hell's going on here. And watch your back, Cabot. We almost lost one agent this summer. One is one too many."

Chapter Twenty-Seven

J ames Roybal paced around his foldout bed in the darkness, hands on hips, trying to get cool. The tiny apartment wasn't all that warm; yet the window air conditioner was struggling. But Roybal was frustrated and furious with himself, the FBI, and Congressman Dawson.

He was angry because first, he'd been sure that staying out of the bank's camera range, on the day of what the FBI agent kept calling "the incident," equaled staying out of the video frame. He hadn't accounted for the marble floor picking up his reflection as he walked to the elevator.

Note to self, he thought, *when I get out of this—and I will, one way or another—I'll pay more attention to the environment.*

Second, when cornered by the FBI, he'd given up easily. He really wasn't happy with himself about that. But damn it, that woman had kept him waiting and filled his head with doomed scenarios about what could happen, and all but threatened to ruin his life if he didn't tell everything. In the back of his mind, he'd imagined that he could withstand pretty much any kind of torture before he cracked. When it came down to it, though, they had him dead to rights, and he'd counted on the fact that the FBI would respect him for doing his patriotic duty, fulfilling the request of an elected member of Congress.

Second note to self: when I get out of this, I will not, under any circumstances, do anything illegal, no matter who asks me.

The crowning blow had come when the FBI released him—with orders to present himself again next week, and a warning that there were flags on his driver's license, license plates and passport—and he'd gone to find

Congressman Dawson.

Figuring out that Dawson's office was in the Rayburn House Office Building was easy. It was pure dumb luck that the Congressman was leaving as Roybal had walked up to the entrance late that afternoon, heading toward his limousine, surrounded by minions.

"Congressman," he called. "I need to talk to you."

One of Dawson's aides held up a hand as if to push Roybal aside.

Dawson himself said, "Make an appointment, son. Call our office on Monday."

Roybal ignored the aide's block. "You might want to know—I was detained by the FBI all day."

The hesitation on Dawson's part, however fleeting, was enough to signal that he'd heard. He scowled. "What's your name?"

"You know damned well what my name is—you have to help me."

Dawson stopped on the sidewalk. "Don't you tell me what I have to do. Unless it's the goddamn President of these United States asking, I don't have to do anything. Now, I don't know who you are. And I have no idea what you want. But you are welcome to call my office and make an appointment, and I guarantee, someone will meet with you if—and only if—you are a resident of the state of Georgia." He turned to his entourage. "Let's go."

The group had closed around him, protective, as if being close to the lawmaker would give them safety as well.

Roybal reeled. "I told them about you. I told the FBI all about you."

Dawson stopped again, but did not look back at Roybal. He merely shook his head and got into the limo.

Roybal cursed himself, Dawson, the whole mess. He'd been foolish to confront Dawson like that, he told himself. What had he expected? That Dawson would admit everything—or anything—in a public place, in front of others?

Third note to self: when I get out of this, if I'm going to discuss secrets, I'll do it in private.

He stood on the sidewalk outside the Rayburn Building for a good five minutes, watched the limo drive off, strode after it and then shuffled back, not knowing what to do.

Marlene Reese saw that obviously no one at the FBI seemed to believe her story about Congressman Dawson, and she was on edge when she returned home Friday night.

After she made herself a sandwich, she poured a glass of wine, turned out the lights, and set a chair in front of her living room window. She closed the drapes so that only a scant gap enabled her to watch the street without being seen.

Dusk was long that night, but once it was truly dark, lit only by a streetlight, Sam's motorcycle hove into view.

She reached into the drawer of a nearby demi-lune table.

Almost before she had her hand out, Sam was at her door, opening it as easily as if it were unlocked. Stepping inside, he looked around and came forward.

"I have a gun, Sam, and I will kill you."

He moved two steps forward, and she spoke again. "Don't be stupid. I'm an old lady defending myself against an intruder."

"You won't shoot."

"I'll shoot, and I won't miss. I practice every weekend—did you know that, Sam? And even if you somehow survive and I don't, you know I've taken precautions." Her voice was deep and level. "Let's say I die, or maybe I'm just injured. Emails will go out, letters will be opened, a whole machine goes into operation that will bring your boss to his knees. I have enough dirt on him that if anything at all happens to me, he will die—alone and sick and penniless." She tsked. "I would have thought he'd think that through before he sent you here."

"He said it was worth the risk."

"It's not. If you leave now, you get to tell him that. If you don't leave now, well, you won't be talking to anyone, will you? I have a 92 magazine that holds fifteen rounds. One of them will hit home. And I know my way around this apartment blindfolded." She chuckled. "So what's it to be? Are you the one who causes the downfall of the great Billy Dawson? Or do you bleed out on the rug, and I get to shop for a new one?"

* * *

Roybal had gone to the gym and put in a heavy workout, but it hadn't helped his mood or his nerves. He was still antsy, angry at the world and mad at himself.

In the darkness now, he parted two of the slats in the blind at the window, looked out at the summer night and promised himself again that he would, really, find a way out of this.

And then he heard the soft click as the door to his apartment opened.

Noiselessly, he withdrew his hand from the blind and pivoted to see the shaft of light from the hallway slice through the darkness in his entryway.

It took him two strides to cross back to where a counter island partly bisected the room. Crouching down, he watched the silhouette of a large man enter and creep the few steps to reach Roybal's foldout bed.

Having spent the last hour in the dark, Roybal could see well enough to determine the intruder wasn't armed. But the intruder could see well enough that the bed was empty.

"What the..." he whispered.

Roybal jumped him.

The intruder crouched, swiveled, and came up at Roybal. He pummeled Roybal in the face and chest; Roybal let go.

Roybal stumbled backwards to the couch. He kept his feet. But he didn't back up to give himself space.

He'd surprised the intruder. He moved in. Counter-attacked.

The intruder defended Roybal's punches. But the move left him open.

Roybal pivoted and threw his left elbow into his attacker's sternum.

The blow rocked the man, briefly. He threw an arm around Roybal's neck and held him in a headlock.

Again, instead of breaking away, Roybal turned close in.

Made a fist. Gave three powerful blows to the man's left side. And felt the ribs crack.

As the man released his chokehold, Roybal spun him, and gave a final, powerful jackhammer blow to the man's left kidney.

The man fell.

Roybal was tempted to kick the broken ribs. He stopped.

Reaching down, he picked the intruder up by his collar and waistband and, staggering, hauled him back to the open door.

Literally throwing the man into the hall, he saw his face clearly for the first time.

Sam. Dawson's goon.

He watched as Sam pulled himself up on the far wall and lurched off down the corridor, clutching his broken ribs.

Turning to go back indoors, Roybal stopped when he saw the couple from next door peek out of their apartment, eyes wide.

"It's over," he said to them. "He won't be back."

Chapter Twenty-Eight

Saturday morning at the YMCA the lifeguard used his whistle at the side of the pool.

Wynn stopped mid-lane, treading water.

"Ms. Cabot," he'd called to her, "your phone's ringing non-stop here." He jerked a thumb over his shoulder. "Somebody wants to reach you, real bad."

Nodding, she ducked under the floating lane dividers, hauled herself out of the pool and hustled to where her phone sat atop a microfiber towel.

Six missed calls—all of them from Linda Grazer.

She shook water from her hair and speed-dialed Grazer.

"Hope you're not too busy," Grazer had answered. "Because here's the deal—that auditor you requested for the Nova Bank case? Yeah, he's dead."

Thinking the wind would dry her hair faster, Wynn tried driving to the condo complex with her head out the window like a spaniel, but the humidity was already high and the temperature climbing. When she pulled up to the guard gate, her curls were still damp. While she made her way to Freund's condo she raked her hair with her fingers.

Presentable, though—if you want me to work on a Saturday, you can't expect salon fresh.

As she approached, Mark Bowles came out the front door of the building, pale and unsteady.

She leaped from the car. "Whoa, sit down before you fall down." She took Bowles' arm and helped him sink onto the single front porch step.

"I'm okay. Not used to seeing dead people, I guess."

"Yeah, right. Your skin is the color of this concrete. Sit for a bit—inhale."

"Thanks." He rested his forearms on his knees and dropped his chin. "I don't know how you all do this. Especially the wo—" He stopped.

"It's our job. Not yours. Why are you even here?"

"I feel responsible."

Wynn nodded. "You asked his help with this investigation, sure. But his death may not even be connected." She turned to go inside. "If it is, help us find the bastard who did it."

Frank Freund's condo held more people that morning than it had held in the entire time Freund had lived there. An FBI Evidence Response Team crawled throughout the condo between a squad from the D.C. Medical Examiner's office, John Byrne from FinCEN, and in the middle of the living room, Linda Grazer stood talking with a petite brunette.

Grazer turned to Wynn, glancing for a moment too long at her wet hair. "Oh, good, you're finally here."

Wynn let the dig pass and extended her hand to the brunette. "Special Agent Wynn Cabot."

The woman returned her firm handshake. "Julie Winters, MPD."

"Nice to meet you, Sergeant. Finally, I can put a face with the name."

"The property manager found the body," Grazer said. "Apparently Freund had requested more files late Thursday, and they were couriered over Friday morning. The guard tried to call Freund, but couldn't reach him, so the courier left the box of files in the guard's kiosk. The manager decided to deliver the box herself this morning. When she let herself in, she found Freund in the kitchen. Called MPD."

"The minute we found out whose condo this was, we called your office," Winters said.

Grazer looked around the room at the activity. "And we brought in the Evidence Response Team and FinCEN. Then the M.E, got here. Hell, our offices are so close together, we all could have carpooled."

Wynn smiled. "And stopped for doughnuts. Do we have anything so far?"

Grazer looked at the notepad on her phone. "The M.E. doesn't have time of death, but it's been at least twenty-four and more like thirty-six hours. Blood had drained to his feet and legs—he was sitting at the kitchen table—rigor's come and gone, the skin is marbled. And the flies are interested but haven't laid eggs yet."

"Cause of death?" Wynn asked.

"Unknown. No visible marks on the body, but the head was..." Grazer put a palm to one side of her chin and pushed.

"When my officers found him his head was twisted on his neck," Winters said. "At an odd angle."

Frowning, Wynn looked around the condo. "We don't know for sure that this has to do with the Nova Bank case."

Grazer and Winters sighed in unison. "True, we don't," Grazer said. "But Freund's computer is missing."

"It's a similar MO to two others I've seen lately," Winters said.

"But this time, the FBI has lost one of our own."

Now it was Wynn's turn to sigh. "Still, it's a first-floor condo. The guard at the gate probably leaves, when? Sundown? Eight o'clock? Anybody could scale the fence or sneak through the gate behind a car."

"Yeah, but who?" Winters raised her shoulders in question. "Did the deceased have any enemies?"

"Of course he did," Grazer said. "He was an auditor. Everybody hates auditors."

Winters arched an eyebrow. "For doing their jobs?"

"Here's the deal. I've worked with Agent Freund off and on for years. He was, well, I liked to think of him as zealous—never more delighted than when he found somebody cooking their books. Even a small math error gave him a big smile. And if you couldn't back up your expense report in detail, he wouldn't hesitate to call your entire accounting department into question, and ruin their careers."

"Sounds like the geek who got pushed around in high school," Wynn said.

"Yeah, but we still have to give this one all we got. Freund was a nasty son of a bitch, but he was *our* son of a bitch. Know what I mean?"

Chapter Twenty-Nine

When Wynn left Freund's condo, she fought with herself about going to the office to check her notes, file new ones, and fill in the details. Mid-July heat made her drowsy, and the supermarket beckoned, but she knew what she needed to do.

Finding a parking spot in the garage near the FBI's entrance was harder to do than she thought it would be on a Saturday. She entered the building and joined the queue at the metal detector and conveyor that were security just inside the door from the parking garage. She chatted with the guards as her line—one of six in and four out—moved forward at a glacial speed. And while she'd relished the air conditioning—also glacial—she still felt the dizzying effects of the midsummer heat.

Which was why, when she saw a familiar-looking man come from the hallway that led to the elevator bank, she thought she was seeing things.

A guard motioned for her to step through the metal detector. As she did, she momentarily lost sight of the figure, thought maybe it was wishful thinking, and then spotted him again.

He looked like André Bishop. Walked like André Bishop—well, like André Bishop would have, if he'd taken a bullet and had broken ribs— It was André Bishop. There was no doubt. He approached the exit kiosks and was badging out, going through the exit procedure.

"André," Wynn called, but in the din he didn't hear her. On impulse, she started toward the exit aisle, but the guard called her back.

"Agent Cabot—your weapon."

She grabbed her gun and handbag off the conveyor and started after Bishop.

"André," she called again. "Don't leave—"

He gave no evidence of hearing her.

Once more, security stalled her as she went through exit procedures. Pushing forward, she fumed. "I need to catch Agent Bishop," she pleaded. "It's important."

Finally through security, she broke free and dashed out the door into the parking garage.

Bishop was nowhere in sight.

Frustrated, she fished in her purse for her phone and thumbed in his speed dial. It rang once and then rolled to voicemail.

The greeting ended, and she spoke softly, trying to calm herself. "André, hi, it's me—Wynn. I just saw you at the office, but couldn't catch you in time. I'm glad to see you're up and around. And I'd like to talk to you—about this case, and well, I just want to know you're okay. Give me a call." Ringing off, she turned back inside to join the security line once again.

* * *

In his car, in a dark corner of the garage, Andre Bishop listened to Wynn's message as he worked his jaw. No, he thought, he wasn't okay. Medically, he was making great progress, but the psych evaluation he'd just received said he needed more time before returning to duty. He didn't feel like talking to anyone right now.

Least of all Wynn Cabot.

That evening, Wynn sat at a table in the Side Hustle, but she might as well have been on top of Denali, as wrapped up as she was in her own thoughts.

Bishop hadn't returned her call, even though she was certain he'd heard her message. Why had he been at the office on a Saturday? Was he back to work the mystery case that no one would tell her about—the one that had gotten him shot? And why wouldn't he call her? Realizing a statement like that made her sound like a jilted lover, she shook her head.

"You're doing it again," said Gio Leo.

"Mmm—sorry, what?"

124

"You're doing it again. I haven't seen you for a month and now that we're together, you're off in la-la-land." Reaching across the table, he took her hand. "What's wrong?"

"Nothing."

He didn't say anything, but let go of her hand.

"I'm sorry. Everything's wrong."

"Talk to me."

"I saw Bishop at the office today."

"He's back. That's great."

"I don't know if he's back. I didn't get a chance to talk to him, and he won't return my call."

"There's a good reason, I'm sure."

"If he can't talk to me about his case, I get it. But I want to ask him about the one I'm working."

"Talk to me," Leo said again. "All you mentioned on the phone was you're working on a stolen sculpture."

"I don't know how much I can tell you, but…" As briefly as she could, Wynn told Leo about the case, and the frustrations of an empty crime scene.

Leo chuckled. "The reason it's called theft is because the object was taken away."

Wynn dipped a finger into her water glass and flicked a drop across the table at him. "It gets weirder. There was a larger theft at the bank—two of them actually…"

She summed up the lack of evidence in the safe deposit box heist—and the fact that the crime scene had been scrubbed and sterilized. Then, she said, she watched surveillance footage that supposedly had nothing conclusive on it, but she'd spotted the reflections in the floor.

"The people in the reflections—we pulled them in, separately, and they both gave us this outrageous story about being commissioned for the theft by a U.S. Congressman, a guy named Dawson."

"Wow."

"Oh, but that's not even the worst. We called in a forensic accounting specialist, and then he was murdered at his condo a couple days ago."

Leo whistled softly. "That *is* weird."

"What's really weird is, the thieves must have known that the FBI would just assign another specialist and keep investigating. So this death can't be related to the case."

"Sure it could," Leo said. "Maybe the thieves are buying time. Maybe they have a side hustle with a big payday around the corner. When that comes in, they'll replace the money or compensate for whatever was stolen."

"Damn," she said. "Does everybody have a side hustle but me?"

"And me." Leo spread his arms. "What you see is what you get. But these days, wages don't go very far, and some people will lie, cheat and steal for luxury goods. The FDA has come across some beauties recently. I've dealt with imitation crab meat, manmade caviar, and we got a guy last week extending coffee with sawdust. I'm telling you, Wynn, all that glitters..."

Glitter, she thought. *Glitter. Where did I see the glitter, and why is it important?*

* * *

She scuffled into her kitchen the following morning, almost remembering what had puzzled her the night before.

She'd been tired when she'd come in, exhausted from the day's events, confused by seeing Bishop and not talking to him, and then her dinner with Gio Leo.

Something she was supposed to remember flitted through her mind again. *The trash bin at the bank,* she thought. *It had glitter in it. Glitter the colors of money: gold and silver. The colors of the elements of the Lowell Chrysler sculpture.*

She closed her eyes and let the dyslexia, which she usually worked to overcome, take over. It brought the sculpture to hang at the forefront of her mind, so that she could walk around underneath it, picturing the precious metal elements that balanced at the end of the platinum arms. *That sculpture shouldn't have had flakes falling off of it at all. Unless...*

She flipped through her case file with one hand and grabbed for her phone with the other. Andy Cardenas at Chrysler's studio would know if there was paint on that mobile.

126

But his phone went to voice mail and instead of leaving a message, she mashed the "end call" icon. Other people had jobs that finished for the week on Friday—hers, not so much.

Hurriedly, she dressed, ran a brush through her hair and grabbed her handbag.

She rolled up to Bishop's condo building in Georgetown and got out of the car. *I need to keep it professional,* she reminded herself. She retrieved a bag of bagels and cream cheese from the front seat. *And yes, we're friends, but no more than that.*

* * *

She caught the locked front door as a resident left and slipped into the building. *Yes,* she thought, *I'm a friend. Making a call on a friend. Because I'm concerned about him. And because I need more balance in my life.*

She knocked on Bishop's door and waited, but heard no movement. She wondered if he was, perhaps, back at HQ, or maybe tucked up in a home office in there, going over files.

She waited and then turned to go.

The door clicked open.

Bishop, clad in plaid Bermuda shorts and a t-shirt, barefoot and unshaven, stood blinking at her.

Retracing her steps, she said, "Morning, Sunshine. I was afraid you were working."

"No. Not today."

"I mean, I saw you at the office yesterday and wondered if you were back at it, working weekends."

"Nope. Yesterday was…follow-up with the suits. You know."

She thrust the bagel bag at him. "I brought some goodies."

Bishop took the bag from her, but didn't move from the doorway.

"Um…do you have coffee?"

He took a deep breath, grimacing when the pain in his ribs bit back. "Maybe another time, Wynn?"

"Everything okay?"

"I don't mean to be rude—" He let out the breath with a sigh. "It's just that there are good days and not-so-good ones. And today's..."

"I'm cool." She held up a hand. "Call me when you feel better."

Disappointed, she went back to her car. A little sad, the way she knew anyone would feel when a sick friend says, "You need to leave now." Respectful, but distant.

Distant—was that it? Did Bishop have a guest he didn't want her to see?

She smiled at the thought, and then smiled at herself for wanting Bishop to have some balance in his life, too.

Closing the door, Bishop stepped to a window and watched her pull away, and then he turned to survey the front room—a wreck of epic proportion, not a hard thing to accomplish in a one-room condo: his bed piled with rumpled sheets and sweat-stained pillows, the small table in the dining area piled with medical supplies, tissues, water bottles and a heap of unopened mail. Clothing, ranging from fresh-from-the-cleaners to dirty laundry, draped the dining area. The pullman kitchen was a mess of dishes, condiment jars and boxes from home-delivery meal kits.

The scent of the place was a mélange of sickroom and locker room.

He surveyed the wreckage and pursed his lips. Maybe the shrink had been right when she'd said he wasn't ready.

Well, if he was going to get better, he needed to act like it: clean first, maybe a little time on the old treadmill to get the blood flowing, and then shower and shave. Maybe wash the car.

He stood up straight, took a lungful of air, and decided to start in the kitchen.

He was halfway across the floor when he realized that, for the first time in a month, it didn't hurt to breathe.

Chapter Thirty

On Monday morning, curious about the way Lowell Chrysler worked, when he still worked, Wynn reached for her phone and scrolled, searching for the number of Wood Creek retirement home in Woodbridge, Virginia, where Chrysler lived. Asking him anything was probably a long shot, she knew, but she needed to know how *Cornucopia* had come together.

"Probably a bad idea," she muttered to herself as she paused at the right number. "Probably think he's talking to a space alien." She jumped when her phone chimed and then she hit the icon to answer the incoming call.

"Agent Cabot, this is the diener from the ME's office in D.C. calling. My boss said you were waiting for autopsy results on Agent Freund?"

"Wait. You're the..."

"Diener. I do the, well, whatever needs to be done to the body for the pathologist to make his findings in cause of death."

"Ah. And what did you...or your pathologist find?"

"Not much, I'm afraid. His neck was snapped, but that we knew. There was bruise DNA, but nothing matching in any of our databases."

"Nothing?"

"I'm afraid not."

"Nothing at all?"

"Nothing. Sorry."

Wynn sighed. Another dead end. She chuckled at her own dark joke, ended the call and hit the number for Wood Creek, dreading another talk with the cantankerous artist. A pleasant-sounding woman answered. Wynn identified herself and asked for Chrysler's room number.

The woman said, "Ah. Excuse me a moment, Agent Cabot," and immediately Wynn heard on-hold music—Bach's "Sleepers, Wake."

Another voice, this one less-cordial, returned to the line. "May I know your credentials, please, Ms. Wynn Cabot?"

Wynn again gave her FBI badge number—D6368KHX—and explained why she wanted to speak to Chrysler.

"Um...official business?"

"Yes, in connection with a recent art theft—the theft of one of Mr. Chrysler's works."

"I see. We have to be careful, you know."

"I know, and I appreciate that. May I speak with Mr. C—"

"That's just the thing, Agent Cabot. Lowell Chrysler died yesterday."

"Died?"

"Yes. And we're not sure why. He was slowly slipping from us mentally, but physically he was quite well. He was aging, of course, but still quite fit. And then, yesterday, he was...gone."

"Do you know where exactly his body is?"

"Of course. Our house physician requested an autopsy. The Medical Examiner's office in Manassas has Mr. Chrysler."

A morning full of autopsy reports wasn't the way she wanted to kick off her week, but she supposed they came with the job. Still, she hadn't expected rapid-fire casualties in the Art Crimes Unit. Two in two days, both suspicious. Wynn sighed. "I'll need the number for the ME in Manassas, if you have it."

"Sadly," the woman said, "we have it on speed-dial. And that's no joke."

Chapter Thirty-One

She needed to talk to someone, to think out loud, but her calls to Bishop kept rolling to voice mail—which was full. Seamus Caine would take her call; she was sure of that.

"What is it?" Caine said.

Wynn smiled. Caine always answered a phone with a snarl. "What is what?"

"Oh, hello, dear. Sorry, I was miles away, mentally. How are things in the art theft business these days?"

"Booming, I'm afraid. Now I'm also involved in the theft of some safe deposit boxes at the same bank the mobile was stolen from."

"Robbing banks is sexy, Wynn. Everyone fantasizes about robbing a bank."

"Probably true, but Nova Bank seems to be a sieve when it comes to security. Listen, I—"

"Any drama? Getaway cars screeching from the scene? Gunplay?"

"None of it."

"How disappointing."

"These were real robberies, Seamus, not Hollywood. Listen, I want to ask you a couple of questions about Lowell Chrysler's work—do you know it?"

"Only what you told me when we talked last, and then a little more. I did some research on him. Very legit."

"Seems Chrysler turned up dead in his retirement home yesterday. Perfectly healthy physically, and then...not so healthy."

"Well, that's certainly dramatic."

Wynn sighed. "I have nothing to go on, except maybe a little glimmer. The mobile at the bank was reputedly silver and gold elements on platinum rods, right?"

"Yes, from what I read. His last piece. His *tour de force* turned *coup de grâce*, eh?"

"Except I don't think it was silver and gold. I think it was painted those colors. And from what the security guard tells me of the way it was disassembled, I think the piece weighed more than it should have, if it were silver and gold. How much do you think it should have weighed?"

"From its depth and breadth I'd say it should have weighed in the neighborhood of two hundred pounds total. The piece was meant to be light enough to move, after all. That's why they're called mobiles."

"So who else makes mobiles?"

"Everyone these days. The Museum of Modern Art sells them in their gift shop—probably made in China. But anyone can fashion a mobile, now that we have lasers that cut metal. Not quite the proposition it was when Alexander Calder was working."

Wynn thought for a moment. She needed to revisit Andy Cardenas in Lowell Chrysler's workshop. "Right," she said. "I need to call you back. I think I have an idea."

Chapter Thirty-Two

Howard Jacobs checked the time on his Rolex Date-just with the diamond bezel—a wedding gift from Sherryl—and winced. He had a pow-wow with the rabbi in an hour. He scrolled through a list of missed calls until he found the number he sought and hit the entry—Congressman B. Crawford Dawson's unlisted phone.

"This better be important," Dawson said by way of greeting.

"It is. You've let this go too far, Dawson. The rabbi's box got looted, and he wants his stuff back. Pronto. I want the stuff back sooner than pronto—anything you can come up with that was taken from his box. And while you're at it, I want my Torah and codex back too. Dammit, that was stupid."

"Listen, I don't have any of what you're calling 'stuff,' Jacobs. And in the future, that'll be 'Congressman Dawson,' to you. Now, I can check with my team to see what they might have, but I wouldn't bet they have anything that resembles a Torah or a whatchamacallit—"

"—codex."

"Yeah, that."

"Now you listen, Dawson—"

"'Congressman' Dawson," Dawson reminded him.

"You won't be 'Congressman' Dawson after this upcoming election if I decide to cut off your…shall we call it your 'allowance,' will you?"

He heard a long pause at Dawson's end of the line. And then Dawson's syrupy drawl: "I don't know that I'll need your help, Jacobs. The campaign coffers are topped up right now, and I have some backup collateral. So I'd

133

suggest you back off with your threats. You're negotiating shit for a guy who's supposed to be such a deal maker."

"I have an appointment with the rabbi in an hour, Dawson, and I—"

"I'm hanging up, Jacobs, if you won't give me some respect."

Jacobs beat him to it. And then he hurled his phone against the nearest wall in a move that was becoming his trademark tantrum.

He slumped into the tufted leather wing chair in his home office, rubbing the back of his neck where the muscles had tightened during his call with the Congressman, while he thought. He had to have something plausible to say to the rabbi—something that wouldn't lose him that seat on the board and would buy him some time to find the Torah and codex—but he couldn't think quite what that might be.

He'd avoided going to Friday night services at the synagogue since the safe-deposit-box heist, but the quarterly meeting of the Temple Board was this evening and the rabbi would be there.

He retrieved his phone from the floor and checked to see if it still worked. Yes. He hit the phone icon and scrolled again through the numbers, finding one he had last dialed a month ago, and hit "call."

After two rings a voice said, "Speak."

Jacobs took a deep breath. "The Torah—our Torah, yours and mine, it's missing."

"Missing?"

"Stolen from a safe deposit box."

"At a bank?"

"Of course, at a bank. At the bank I own."

"I'm sure the bank has insurance that will cover it, don't you?"

"Um, no. No, banks don't insure the contents of safe deposit boxes."

"Never?"

"No. If you want your belongings insured, you have to be sure they're covered on your homeowners' insurance."

"Do you think people know that?"

"No. Most people don't know that. It says so on the agreement they sign when they rent a box, but people don't read those things. So, I'm wondering if you've heard anything about where the Torah might…"

"Not me, my friend, but I'll put out the word."

"Quietly, eh? It shouldn't get back to my rabbi that it's missing."

"Oh no?"

"I'd given the Torah to the temple, and then they asked me to store it in their deposit box at—"

"—your bank. You're a real fool, Jacobs."

"That may be, but I have to find that Torah. And its codex."

The man on the other end of the line moaned. "The codex too? *Mein gott, mein gott in himmel,* you *schlemiel.*" He sighed. "I'll try. But if I find them, their return, with nothing said to your rabbi, will run you another twenty thousand."

Jacobs swallowed hard. He had the money, that wasn't the point. The point was the extortion. "Done," he said. "Done. Call me when you find them."

"If," the man said. "Not when. If."

"Twenty thousand is a powerful motivator, I would think. I'd like to have them back this week."

But he had spoken those words into a dead line.

Chapter Thirty-Three

The smell of chlorine assaulted Wynn's nose as she stood in the chin-deep water, clutching the side of the pool. The YMCA's Late Nite Adult Swim was exactly what she needed after a long, confusing day, she decided, and some laps would work out the kinks in her neck and shoulders.

If not the kinks in this case.

Pulling her knees up in front of her, she put her feet against the pool wall and pushed off backward, arms arcing as she shot into the lane.

She shifted into the powerful rhythm of her backstroke, considering the stages of the case as she swam.

First, there was the theft of the sculpture. Whoever took it must have known the theft would be discovered; you don't waltz off with a high-profile piece like *Cornucopia* and expect that no one will notice when it doesn't come back.

She reached the opposite end of the pool, arched her torso forward and kicked off again, to do the next lap in an Australian crawl.

Then there was the safe deposit box theft. What the Bank Theft agents called a Double Whammy. The break-in was so brazen, so blatant, it couldn't be anything else. And what a fantastic story James Roybal and Marlene Reese told—had they concocted this tall tale together at some point? Because they each said exactly the same thing, even though they'd been interviewed separately. So either it was a story they invented and agreed on ahead of time… Or it was true.

She couldn't accuse a sitting Congressman of bank robbery, even these days, just on the say-so of two people.

Reaching her starting point, she dived down, pushed off with her feet again and resumed her backstroke.

But a Double Whammy? The heist's victims must have known the heist was going down, so they could remove the contents of their deposit boxes ahead of time, and then claim the thefts on their insurance. In a Double Whammy, the whole idea is that the theft is discovered.

More important was what Mark Bowles and Frank Freund had been working on—the missing money. Bowles had filed Suspicious Activity Reports and had, at one time, had emails and photos that might've been useful, but those had vanished, and FinCEN's copies of the SARs had disappeared as well. Who had them?

Most important was Freund's death. She didn't know how that could possibly be related to the audit of Nova Bank; killing Freund wouldn't stop it.

Might slow it down, though.

The FBI, of course, had already assigned another auditor to investigate the inconsistencies outlined in the SARS. But the new man—or woman—would need a day or two to get up to speed on the case.

If Freund's killing was connected to Nova Bank—which was still a big if, in her mind—the perpetrators must have known it would buy them, at most, forty-eight hours before the audit would continue.

The thieves must have known that.

Must have known.

Must have known.

Must have known.

It was a pattern—but a pattern of what?

She stopped in mid-lane, treading water. What was happening here?

And how would she find out?

"Dive into the middle, and swim toward the edge," she told Grazer the next day.

"Good," Grazer said, taking a sip from her coffee as she stood at Wynn's desk. "I was afraid you might figure it out too quickly, but I see I needn't have worried."

Wynn tensed. The criticism was true, if unwelcome. "I figure we start over with the safe deposit box heist—the Double Whammy. I want to review what it was, exactly, that was taken from those boxes."

"You have the lists?"

"We know which boxes were drilled out—we could see that at the crime scene. Then I got a list of the box holders from Marlene Reese's file." She held it up. "I've tried contacting them, but they're either MIA or don't want to say what was in their boxes."

"Keep after them. Because here's the deal—if they cleaned out those boxes beforehand, and then claimed the contents were stolen in the heist, it's insurance fraud."

"How do we prove that, though?"

"Figure it out," Grazer snapped. "I need to start hearing some results on this." She waved her empty coffee mug at Wynn and walked away.

Wynn sat back in her chair, stretching her arms overhead, and then lowered her hands to the desktop. One hand fell on the list of boxes, and the other on the list of box holders.

There was no magic in the numbers assigned to the boxes and, presumably, no connection among the box holders. How could she find out what was in those boxes? She had no leverage with these people.

Or did she?

Of all the people on the list, there were two she could pressure if she needed to: Jacobs and Summers.

She tried Jacobs first. The maid answered Jacobses home number, and said Mr. Jacobs was not in, but that she would leave a message. Jacobs' cell number immediately went to voice mail. Wynn left a terse message and her number. Obviously, Howard Jacobs was incommunicado for a while.

Summers, then, she thought. Reaching him at the bank, she heard again his diatribe—part lecture on why she should be chasing "real criminals" and part lecher on why she should become his "special friend"—for a full minute before she interrupted.

"Mr. Summers, what was in your safe deposit box?"

"I, ah, what?"

"It's a simple question. The contents of your safe deposit box. That you claim were stolen."

"I claim they were stolen because they were stolen. My wife's necklace. Diamonds and rubies and emeralds and so forth."

And tastefully understated, I'm sure, Wynn thought. "And I assume you've filed the claim with your insurance company?"

"Headware Insurance. Yes, of course."

She gave him cursory thanks, hung up, and dialed Anton Headley at Headware.

"Ms. Cabot. Any word on the missing mobile?"

"I'm calling about something else today, Mr. Headley. Mr. Summers tells me his wife's necklace was stolen from their safe deposit box."

His sigh was audible through the phone. "Again, I cannot comment on an active claim."

"Mr. Headley, you were supposed to call me back last week and you didn't. Now, I can subpoena your files and bring the Insurance Commission down on you like a hurricane in the Caribbean, or you can tell me what I need to know. Your choice."

The silence lasted twelve seconds—she counted—before he answered. "It was bespoke, gemstones in white gold, a custom made suite by Steeper Designs."

Wynn's eyebrows shot up. Steeper Designs, known to the working class as Steeper Prices, was top shelf.

At length Headley spoke. "If I may be candid, Ms. Cabot? Paying out these claims...well, it could be the end of Headware."

"I'm just trying to get at the truth, Mr. Headley." Thanking him for the information, she rang off and called Steeper.

Two minutes of identifying herself—again by job title and badge number to various levels of minions, and she was talking to Garth Steeper himself, the man who'd designed the necklace.

"I remember it, yes," he said. "God, what a mess. I designed a simple, elegant necklace and earrings. Mrs. Summers loved the simplicity of it, but

Mr. Summers kept wanting to hang more stuff off of it, you know? Like if she waved it, she could stop a train. They had a pitched battle right here in the studio—I walked out and left them to fight."

Wynn giggled. "Let me guess. She won?"

"Yeah, of course." Steeper laughed with her. "I'll email you a photo."

"That'd be great," she said. "And...not to be insulting, but was it real gemstones?"

"Yeah, it was. Totally. I don't do paste and I don't scam anybody."

His comment jogged her thought process. "If I wanted to have a copy made, where would I go?"

He made a sound like sucking through his teeth. "Probably you'd want to go to one of the workshops in Baltimore. I have a couple numbers here somewhere. I'll text you those, along with a photo of the pieces."

Twenty minutes later she had it up on her screen, clucking at how the pieces actually were tastefully done, and how she had misjudged based on Summers' description. She wondered how often Summers and his wife disagreed on things. But she had a hunch who won, every time.

The real pay dirt, though, she found when she dialed the second workshop number Steeper had sent in his text.

"Yes, yes," said the man on the other end of the line in a thick foreign accent. "Yes, I remember this well. A perfect copy we made. Using only the finest synthetic materials."

Which are still synthetic, Wynn thought. "Do you have a photograph you can send me?"

"But yes—I am proud to show you my work."

"It might be used in a legal case."

He gave a sharp intake of breath. "But I have done nothing wrong—it is not to break the law, these copies. It is to protect people from thieves."

"I know," Wynn said, hoping to placate him; she couldn't afford to lose him at this point. "I know."

"We obey the law," he said. "We do many favors for the gentlemen at Nova Bank. But no, we do not break the law."

"I'm sure not," she said.

Chapter Thirty-Four

After talking to the knockoff jeweler who made the copy of Mrs. Summers' necklace, Wynn called Summers back, saying she'd tracked down the paste version.

"I did have a paste version made," he said. "Meredith wears that one when she goes out. The real one we kept in the safe deposit box at the bank."

"Tell you what," Wynn said, "we need you here at FBI HQ this afternoon to answer a few more questions."

"This afternoon is out. I have a lot—"

"This afternoon, Mr. Summers. If I have to, I will send agents to get you. If you come on your own, it will count in your favor."

"If it won't take too long."

"Oh, and Mr. Summers, when you come, please bring that paste version of your wife's necklace."

* * *

Summers appeared at the Hoover Building, indignant and insecure, half anger and half bluster, and sat at a table across from Wynn in a room with a two-way mirror. The necklace lay on the table between them.

Dark sweat patches in the armpits of his blue dress shirt grew larger over the course of the conversation, although the FBI interview room thermostat read a government-approved seventy-four degrees.

The atmosphere, and the conversation, were decidedly chilly.

In the next room, on the other side of the mirror, Mark Bowles stood next to Linda Grazer. "I don't get it," he said. "What's she going on about the necklace for?"

"You'll see."

"I spent months compiling the financial data and filing the SARS. She wants to bust him for a fake necklace?"

"Cool your jets, Bowles. She'll get there."

"I could do a better job. I'm going in there—"

"No, you're not. It's her case. If I decide she's not up to it, I'll be the one to take her off it. But right now, she's the one in there."

Wynn Cabot, though, wasn't finding any joy being the one in there yet, because the one in there with her was being deliberately obtuse.

It must be deliberate, she decided. He's a bank president. He can't be stupid.

"I mean," Summers said, "anybody can see, it's a cheap copy. The jewels don't sparkle and the settings don't shine."

"It looks nice to me," said Wynn.

"Yeah, Meredith likes it too. I told her, she could've had twice the bling, but she likes it this way."

A soft knock interrupted them, and the door opened as an agent in shirtsleeves entered. Wynn handed him the necklace.

Summers sprang to his feet. "Hey!"

"Relax," she said. "He's not going anywhere with it."

He wasn't. He held the necklace in one hand and with the other the agent put a jeweler's loupe up to his eye and examined the stones.

Summers sat again. "That's not a valid test," he said. "Any more, you can't tell the good fakes from the real thing, not with a magnifying glass."

"Actually, he can."

"But that's...but that's not...you don't..." Summers stopped.

The agent dropped his loupe in a shirt pocket, pulled out a phone and tapped in eight digits. Turning the screen to Wynn, he smiled.

"Uh huh," Wynn said. "Mr. Summers, good news. The stones are real. The diamonds have ID numbers on them." She took the necklace back from the agent, who left, closing the door. Eyeing Summers, Wynn added, "You don't seem very happy about that."

"I don't see how it could be," he answered. "Meredith must have got this one mixed up with the fake last time she wore it and gave me the wrong one to put into the safe deposit box."

"Well, in any case, you have the real thing, so you won't need to file that insurance claim." She pushed the necklace across the table at him.

With his fingertips, he worked the necklace toward him until his fist closed over it. "So I guess I can leave, then." He rose.

"Oh, sit down, Mr. Summers." Wynn opened a file beside her. "We're just getting warmed up." She looked through the top few pages. "As a matter of fact, you're quite good at having fakes made, aren't you?"

"Come again?"

"You had a paste copy made of the *Cornucopia* sculpture, didn't you?"

"I— of course not. I never—"

"Yeah, I have to ask, was there ever a real one, in that case? Because the one hanging in your bank was a fake all along, wasn't it?"

"That's crazy." He leveled a finger at her. "You're accusing me of, of—I'll have your job for this."

"No worries, it's my job to make accusations." She closed that file and reached for another. "It's easy enough to find out who made that knockoff, too. But let's talk about some really big fakes." Leafing through the second file, she smiled. "Like the fake loans you made to a friend of yours."

The color drained from his face. "Y-you don't know what you're talking about."

Wynn put her elbows on the table and leaned across. "Sure I do. Remember our auditor? Between Mr. Freund and Mark Bowles we've pieced together what we need."

In the room behind the mirror, Mark Bowles exhaled, pleased, at least until he heard Summers' reply over the intercom:

"I want my attorney."

Bowles ruffled his hair. He'd known a fight was coming, but all the same, he'd hoped Summers would confess.

"Damn," was all Bowles said.

An hour later, Linda Grazer led Wynn and Mark Bowles into her office. She parked one hip on

the desk top, swinging her free leg.

"All right," she said. "He called for his lawyer, the lawyer will put him on a choke chain with a muzzle and he'll be out of here by the end of the day. I'd like to keep him here and coerce him—purely, of course, in the interest of justice—convince him to help us sort out this mess. But we can't. So where does that leave us?"

"Beginning at the end," Wynn said. "We've got him on loan fraud."

"We will have him on loan fraud," Bowles said, "as soon as we link the loan documents back through the audit and trace the money to the individual bank accounts."

"Make sure you do," Grazer said. "Because here's the deal. That slick lawyer will have him silent as a cadaver with a grudge. He won't give us anything. It's going to be all on us to get the minute details on this one."

"We will," Bowles said. "We need signoffs on the subpoenas to examine those accounts."

Grazer stood. "I'm handling the subpoena for Dawson's."

Wynn sat in one of Grazer's guest chairs. "It really peeves me that we can't tie Summers to the safe deposit theft." She shook her head. To her mind, Summers didn't seem smart enough to be a bank president, and he let his human appetites—all of them—lead him. Those things alone made him obnoxious, but they also made him easy to manipulate. Anyone who fed his ego could command Peter Summers, but that kind of feeding took money and influence.

Grazer leaned again on her desk, thinking out loud. "We're not clear what part Summers played in the safe deposit heist, if any. Maybe he was just being stupid. Maybe he actually did put the wrong necklace back in the box."

"He's involved. He must be," Bowles said. "But what about the sculpture? That's more your wheel house than mine."

Wynn rubbed the back of her neck. "This case has more knots than my shoulder muscles right now."

"No kidding. If the sculpture they took down back in June was a fake, then it isn't really a—" Grazer waggled her index fingers in single air quotes—"major art crime, is it? If it was a bunch of painted wood and electrical conduit, running off with it is barely a misdemeanor."

Wynn took a deep breath. "I disagree. Lots of artists have concepts carried out with everyday materials. Jackson Pollock worked with house paint and canvas."

"But Chrysler's idea was to make a statement about wealth and fortune with precious metals."

Wynn nodded. "Now that he's dead, we may never know. We speculate that's what he was doing."

"And the bank perpetuated that notion," Bowles said.

"True," Wynn admitted. "They didn't say anything to the contrary."

Chapter Thirty-Five

The next morning Wynn breezed into the office juggling two coffees. She set them on her desk just as Grazer's toady appeared, his face ashen.

"Agent Cabot..."

She flashed him a smile, knowing what was coming.

"...there's a visitor for you—a VIP visitor—in Conference Room C."

"Ah, yes," she said. "That'll be Senator Osborne."

Osborne stood at the head of the conference table in an impeccable summer-weight wool suit.

Wynn set the two green-and-white cups on the table. "I'm glad I caught you before you got the office joe. Life's too short to caffeinate with the cheap stuff." Motioning for him to sit, she took an adjoining chair.

He reached into his inner jacket pocket. "How's Bishop?"

Wynn's face clouded. "Injured in the line of duty, out of action for a while. Back at work just this week."

"Wow. Glad to hear it. I'll have a word with him before I leave." Osborne withdrew a flash drive from his pocket and then covered it with a hand. "Agent Cabot, about that footage you asked me for."

She cocked her head. "Do I sense a problem?"

He closed a fist around the drive. "Actually, a couple of problems."

"Okay..."

"First, any footage from government cameras is classified. It's to be viewed by certain people only, and it wouldn't be admissible in court."

Letting out a low whistle, she shook her mop of curls. "Ah. That could be tough."

He nodded. "Second, I would have had to pull rank, not to mention a few strings, to get video like that."

"That's why I asked you. I have no rank and no strings."

"Exactly. I know you're new. But how things work, here in Washington…"

"Mm. You would need a quid pro quo in return?"

"You're a fast learner." He held the drive out to her. "So you realize, I can't give it to you."

"No." She reached for the drive, pulled her hand back, and then reached out again, took the thumb drive from him, dropped it in her empty coffee cup and replaced the cup lid. "I'll have to go a different route, then." She smiled up at Osborne. "I'll get it from one of my sources. Who must, of course, remain unnamed, for reasons of national security."

Osborne grinned. "I'm hoping you can find someone to help you out… when I could not." He rose. "Thanks, I'm glad we had this chat."

He studied her face for a moment and stepped to the door. Opening it, he glanced across the room, spotting André Bishop at his desk. "I'll pay my respects to Agent Bishop on my way out."

* * *

Throughout the morning co-workers had stopped by André Bishop's desk to tell him how glad they were to see him or how relieved they'd been to hear he'd survived. A few hadn't heard and wanted to know if he'd been on vacation.

For his part, Bishop felt a mix of gratitude, relief, and doubt as he sat there—grateful, of course, for the medicos who kept him alive in those critical first hours after he was shot—he'd never be able to express how grateful. Relieved to be back at work at last, even though he doubted all that lay ahead, he was unsure he would be physically and mentally able to cope with the rigors of FBI life again.

Finding his footing at the office would be the least of it, although people skills had never been his long suit. Reconnoitering what happened the night he was shot would be job one—and he wondered if reliving those moments would trigger some PTSD. And then, oh lordy, there was getting reacquainted with Wynn.

He wasn't sure why, exactly, he'd kept her apprised of his whereabouts during his long trip out of Israel, but he felt someone—some friendly face in the U.S.—should know where he was, in case…well, just in case. She seemed to be the only one concerned enough to contact him, so she got the nod.

Now, however, now that he was faced with working with her again, he wasn't comfortable with her, not that he'd ever been completely comfortable around her, but this felt different. More…personal.

And then Jake Osborne showed up at his desk, resting his leather briefcase atop a stack of case files.

Bishop tried to stand, winced, and grabbed for his ribs. Dammit. Full recovery was going to take longer than he wanted. The docs had warned that it might. Bishop wanted life to get back to normal.

"Please," Osborne said, "don't try to stand."

"Senator," he said. "How're things on the Finance Committee?"

"I'm chairing Intel now, thanks to my predecessor's…uh…retirement."

"I hadn't heard."

Osborne sat in the guest chair next to Bishop's desk. "I understand the Middle East wasn't altogether kind to you."

"I've had better trips."

"So I heard. Just quickly, I met with your Agent Cabot for a few minutes. She's tangling with people she shouldn't be, you know."

"I've seen Agent Cabot handle herself when she's tangling with people she shouldn't be. That's why I offered her this job."

"These people are different," Osborne said.

"Wynn has dealt with corrupt and ambitious people before."

Osborne lowered his voice. "Sitting where I am, I'm privy to things you may not be. There's deep intel. These people, Bishop, they're more like the folks you encountered in Jerusalem."

Bishop raised an eyebrow. "Ah. Okay, I'll let her know. Honestly, I've been out of the loop for so long, I'm not even sure what Agent Cabot is bird-dogging."

"On another topic, I need you to do me a favor."

"If I can."

"You can," Osborne said. "I'm asking that you and Agent Cabot go after Billy Dawson with everything you've got."

"Congressman Dawson?"

"The same. Dawson is pitching—pitching hard—to be nominated to run as VP. The convention is coming up in a couple of weeks, and...."

"And?"

"So far it looks like Dawson's got the nod." Osborne sighed. "But he's also got something going on with Nova Bank—that's the angle Agent Cabot is working—and it's something more than collecting a six-figure salary for being a figure-head on their board. This goes deeper than any of us can imagine, I think." He stood and picked up his leather briefcase. "Anyway, throw everything you've got at Dawson. I'd—well, Colette, would be grateful."

"Colette?"

"Behind every successful man and all that, eh? Colette thinks I should be VP. Well, she thinks I should be President, but she'll settle for being Second Lady. She's already got her inauguration duds picked out. If Dawson goes down, I'm next in line for the VP nomination. The convention is the end of August, Bishop. Colette would be grateful to be on that stage."

Bishop watched the elevator doors behind Osborne. He was vaguely aware of what Wynn was working on—Linda Grazer had briefed him when he first arrived at Walter Reed, but he was so loopy on pain killers he could remember only bits and pieces. Wynn did seem to have a knack for finding more trouble than she'd bargained for, first in Santa Fe, and then in the Napa Valley, and now here in D.C. As though trouble followed her.

He grabbed up a tablet and pen and rose gingerly from his chair.

"Morning," he said as he approached her desk.

Wynn looked up and brightened. "Good morning, yourself. You're looking better. Welcome back."

Bishop settled slowly into the chair beside her desk. "I have a short meet with Linda in a few minutes—can you bring me up to speed on what's cooking?"

Wynn leaned back in her chair and picked up her notes.

"First, I have to ask," Bishop said, "how it is Jake Osborne knew I was in Jerusalem?"

"What?"

"He just said he knew I was in Jerusalem."

"I swear, André, I didn't tell him. I said you'd been shot, but I didn't say where it happened."

"I didn't think you would. The remark struck me as odd. And then he told me he wants us to go after Congressman Dawson with both barrels."

Wynn chuckled. "That may be the only way we can get B. Crawford Dawson to listen. Here's what's cooking..."

From his office at the Rayburn House Office Building, Billy Dawson dialed the private number he had for the head of the Republican National Committee. She answered on the first ring.

"Billy D. here, Madam Chairwoman, returning your call. Are you somewhere where you can talk?"

"I am."

"I understand there is a problem with my nomination?"

"A hiccup, let's say, Congressman. We've discovered, in our vetting process, that you have some problems concerning your association with Nova Bank. You've been taking a salary for sitting on their board? Christ on a coke binge, Dawson—you know that's unethical."

Dawson swallowed hard and thought. "I...I needed the money for the campaign. I can pay it back and apologize to the ethics committee—would that smooth things over?"

"I hear there are other problems in the pipeline."

"Nothing we can't handle, if you can call off the FBI, Madam Chair. Can you get them off my back?"

"Not altogether, Billy. I can get them to slow walk it maybe, until after the election. That's the best we can hope for."

Throughout Wynn's brief meeting with Bishop, he seemed brusque. She filled him in on the case, hitting the major points, but his thousand-yard stare made it clear he wasn't interested in what she'd found out, much less the details.

She popped the lid off her coffee cup, pulled out the thumb drive and shoved the drive into a port on her laptop. "Want to watch footage with me?"

Bishop winced and demurred.

And when she asked him about his own case, he stood and said, "Later," made an awkward pivot, and took off for Grazer's office.

She still couldn't get a read on how well he might be coping with his injuries: obviously he was still hurting, and who knew what being shot had done to his psyche? Even after firearms training at Quantico, she didn't have a real idea of what being shot was like, though she'd heard that it hurt more than you thought it would—and that being shot messed with your head.

* * *

The footage began with the pre-dawn darkness of E Street, the camera aimed at the curb. A lone security guard stood at the front of the mysterious office building to the left of the screen. In the right of the frame, the arches of Nova Bank's parabolic structure loomed like ghostly origami.

She stared at dim images on the screen, seeing little of interest; this was footage from the day of the sculpture theft; so much had happened since then. Speeding up the frames-per-second did little to alleviate the tedium.

Her mind drifted. Osborne had made it clear she'd be expected to expend some effort on his behalf. What he would possibly demand, she had no idea.

As the sun rose in the video on her screen, the images grew clearer, but the only activity was in Wynn's mind. Osborne showed no interest in her personally, so a dalliance was, thankfully, out of the question. That left professional doings. *What could I do*, she wondered, *to help a powerful U.S. Senator—*

And there it was.

On the screen, the big box truck that Versailles must have used, pulling up in front of the bank and making a three-point turn in the street, maneuvering its rear loading door closer to the sidewalk. And aimed directly at the surveillance camera. All she had to do was…

Damn.

Its license plate was covered with mud.

Hunching over her keyboard, she inched her nose closer to the screen and watched.

Grazer's voice cut through Wynn's concentration. "What are you looking at?"

Wynn jerked upright. "Footage of E Street, the day the Nova Bank sculpture was stolen."

"You get that from Jake Osborne? I heard he came to see you."

Wynn looked straight at Grazer. "From a source." Not a lie, not technically.

"Anything on it?"

Turning back to her computer, Wynn watched the Versailles crew unload a man-lift. "Not yet."

"Here's the deal—Bishop may be back, but he's working his own case. I want to be kept up to speed on yours. You find anything, you tell me. Don't filter it through Bishop—he has his hands full. I want to hear directly. Yes?"

"Yes, ma'am." As Grazer moved on to another agent's desk, Wynn's focus again moved close to the screen: the Versailles crew moved wide, flat pieces of lumber, the man-lift, and moving blankets into the bank. From time to time, they came out, each with a bundle in his arms, each loading his bundle into the back of the truck and returning to the building for the next piece of the sculpture.

Finally, they brought out the long arms of *Cornucopia*, followed by the mechanical lift and the boards. The loading done, the crew piled in the cab. A man with a long beard appeared, checked the area, and slammed the truck's rear doors.

Just enough vibration to knock the mud from the license plate.

Wynn clicked Pause and used two fingers on the screen to enlarge the image. She could read most of it, probably enough. Writing the number with one hand, she groped for her phone with the other and dialed an FBI extension.

"Hey, it's Wynn Cabot. I need somebody to run a local plate for me."

Idly clicking around on her computer while she thought about the case, Wynn deleted a month's worth of old emails, shopped for nothing in particular on Amazon, and checked her Instagram account to see if her mother had posted anything recently. She switched back to email. Something from a home furnishings website and an email from Gio Leo. She'd read that one later—she was in no mood to go out.

She absently clicked on her spam file and gasped. Among the dross was a message from Frank Freund, dated and timed to just before he died.

Cautiously she moved her mouse over the email, wondering whether the message was real, or a virus cleverly disguised as something someone knew she'd want to read. There was nothing in the subject line, nor was there any message in the body of the email other than a Power Point attachment.

She held her breath, opened the attachment, and jumped to her feet when she saw Freund's diagram of Summers' scheme. Each box related to the ones above it and below it, explaining how Summers had moved money out of and back into the bank after it was laundered.

Perhaps Freund hadn't realized it, but what he'd drawn resembled...a mobile.

She unplugged her laptop and headed for Grazer's office.

Grazer leaned in, studying the diagram on Wynn's screen, only half intent on what she was seeing. She was bothered, more, by a phone call she'd received early that morning from the chairman of the Republican National Committee, a woman who didn't engage in pleasantries before she got to the point of the call: that Grazer's investigators should back off any enquiry of Congressman B. Crawford Dawson.

Grazer had questions—what investigation? Why would the RNC be calling with instructions such as these? Who had put a bug in the RNC's ear that Dawson was even on the FBI's radar?

The official from the RNC wasn't interested in talking further. Have a nice day, she'd said. And then silence.

Grazer straightened and pushed away Wynn's laptop. "Have a seat, Cabot. I've got some bad news."

The vibe had felt off all morning, Wynn thought as she sat across from Grazer.

She was about to be fired, she was sure. Not including Grazer in her meeting with Jake Osborne was out of line, she knew. Doing an end-run on Grazer to find, and then stay in contact with, Bishop was out of line too.

"Here's the deal," Grazer said. "The RNC wants us to shut down any investigation of Congressman Dawson."

"But Freund's report, and Roybal—"

Grazer held up a hand to stop her protest. "I know, I know what Freund's report means, and I know what Roybal said. But somehow, this got out. Have you been talking out of turn, Cabot? Think—said something to anyone outside the bureau?"

Wynn's mind raced. Had she mentioned something about the case to anyone? Anyone? This was the second time this morning she'd been asked—almost accused—of giving information to outside sources, first by Bishop, and now Grazer.

"I can't think that I did…"

Grazer came out from behind her desk to stand over Wynn. "The book on you, Cabot, is that you don't think."

Wynn tensed. "I don't think?"

"What did you think," Grazer waggled fingers in air quotes, "you were doing by trying to see him? Did you realize you might be blowing his cover?"

"Bishop never said he—"

"When I told you to stay clear of Bishop, I meant *stay clear*. Period. But you decided you knew better."

"I was concerned for—"

"That's not part of your job, Cabot, to be concerned for a fellow agent. I'll do the worrying around here—that's what I'm paid for. You're paid to do exactly as I say. Yes?"

Wynn stared at her hands in her lap, trying to remember if she'd mentioned anything—*anything*—to anyone about the case.

Grazer leaned in to look at her face. "*Yes?*"

"Yes."

Grazer straightened and went back to her desk. "Make that 'yes, ma'am.'"

"Yes, ma'am."

CHAPTER THIRTY-FIVE

"So here's the deal—I'll take over investigating Dawson."

Wynn sat silent, her teeth clenched.

"Do you understand, Cabot?"

"Yes."

"Yes…" Grazer prompted.

"Yes, ma'am."

"You'll hand over everything that mentions Dawson's name. Your job—the only job you have now—is to investigate Peter Summers. It is not to interfere in what Bishop is doing or anything else. Yes?"

Wynn sighed. "Yes, ma'am."

"If anyone mentions Dawson from here on out, you involve me, yes? And I'll tell you the same thing I told Agent Bishop this morning—you're both on probation for six months."

Linda Grazer stared at the notes on her desk. Something niggled at her—the conflict she had about Dawson's part in all of this, or, rather, his lack of any part in all of this. Added to that, the fact that the RNC thought it was important to call her off of any investigation she might be pursuing that involved him. All that did was ring alarm bells, so far as she was concerned. If the RNC knew something was up with Dawson, then something was up. But what?

They had the crazy story that Roybal told about him. And it was common knowledge that Dawson sat on Nova Bank's Board of Directors, for which he received a dandy sum—better money for a cameo stint than Grazer made working full time in a year.

Bishop had told her that Osborne wanted the FBI to dig up everything they had on Dawson, because Dawson was queued up to be the next Vice President if the Republicans had their way about things in November. Osborne clearly wasn't privy to the RNC's request that she call off the dogs.

She had nothing but a hunch. And she wouldn't have even had that had it not been for the call from the RNC.

Something had to give in all of this. And the answer was to go after Dawson full bore, RNC be damned.

Still smarting over her dust-up in Grazer's office, Wynn drove out to the address MPD had listed for the plate on the truck in the surveillance tape. She went by herself, and without a warrant. She hoped one wouldn't be necessary, that she could do this alone, and that she'd find the sculpture—real or bogus—without one, bringing that part of the case to closure.

In his seedy clapboard house near a rail yard, the titular head of Versailles Art Transport who once resembled ZZ Top's Billy Gibbons, sat on his lumpy, threadbare sofa. "This is a temporary living situation," he said. "I'm sure you understand." He leaned back and draped his arms along the back of the sofa. "Yep, people in our line of work, you and me, from time to time we need to work *sub rosa*." He rubbed his now-clean-shaven chin.

Wynn raised an eyebrow. "*Sub rosa*."

"Incognito. Under the radar. In disguise." He rotated his head as if to loosen his neck muscles. "Oh, yeah. I work for people in the highest echelons." He hunched forward. "The highest."

"Who hired you to steal the sculpture?"

"No one."

"I have you on camera, loading it into your truck—" She knew the footage wasn't admissible, but she had to pressure this oddball somehow.

"No one hired me to steal it, Agent Cabot. They hired me to take it down and dispose of it."

"Fine. Who hired you to take it down?"

"Nova Bank."

She paused. That was the official answer. "That wasn't what I asked. Someone at the bank hired you?"

"I'd need to check to make sure it's okay—"

"We can do this here, or we can take a ride."

"I've always wanted to see the inside of that building."

"You can't answer my question, can you?"

"You can't intimidate me with your interrogation, Ms. Cabot. I'm protected by my employer. I said the same thing to the men who came by yesterday."

"What men?"

"Let's say, employees of a powerful legislator."

"Don't tell me. B. Crawford Dawson."

His surprise was instant, and genuine. "Oh, hell no." He snorted a laugh. "You got it all backwards. But then, FBI does that a lot, don't they?" His right leg began to bounce up and down. "Hell, I'll tell you, then. Dawson's the one who hired me to take down the sculpture. The goons yesterday were from Jake Osborne's office."

It was Wynn's turn to be surprised. *Of course, Osborne would have seen the footage. Of course he would have had MPD run the plate, and would've sent someone to interview this guy. Osborne knew everything before he gave me the thumb drive this morning.*

"Where's the sculpture now?"

"In a Maryland landfill, I imagine. We stashed it in a roll-off at a construction site."

"So the mobile wasn't made of precious metals, then?"

"Totally bogus. The paint was bubbling off, the steel connector rods were rusted...the whole thing would have fallen down on some unsuspecting coupon-clipper sooner or later."

"Why were you in disguise the day you took down the mobile?"

"Don't you use different personas when you work? That beard was one of mine. I tell you, though, two weeks ago it saved my life. Guy came up behind me, grabbed my chin and tried to twist my head off." He laughed. "I took off and all he got was a handful of fake beard."

Wynn's dinner fork was halfway to her mouth when the day's adrenaline finally ran out and exhaustion took over.

She sat at the desk in her second bedroom she'd converted to an office, a plate of takeout curry and samosas in front of her. A corkboard on the wall boasted photos, sticky notes and a reminder for a dentist's appointment. To her left, in a shelving unit, were books, a few small art pieces she'd salvaged from her divorce. Behind her, on the floor, a cardboard box held swimming medals and trophies she hadn't bothered to haul out for display.

She lowered her fork. The curry was getting cold anyway, and she reckoned it probably wasn't a good idea to eat spicy food this late at night. Wiping her hands on a napkin, she nudged the plate aside, took a drink of mango lassi, pulled her notebook computer out of her briefcase and opened it on the desk.

There was much to be glad about, she knew, now that they could move forward with Summers' involvement in the loan fraud. But something felt out of place, not fully formed, still incipient in her head. She'd hoped that dynamiting Summers' other stories—his lame excuse about his wife's necklace and the lulu of a tale about the sculpture—would have brought about a confession, or at least some information that would clear up the whole mess.

Something still nagged at the back of her brain, something she'd missed along the way or knew and then forgot she knew.

Arching her back, she rolled her chair to the bookshelf, reached into a basket, grabbed three shrink-wrapped pads of sticky notes, each in a different neon color, and twisted them open. She took up a pen and wrote, adhering the notes to the surface of the desk.

The first batch, chartreuse, she used for notes about the sculpture: Versailles Art Restoration, Chrysler (now dead), his studio, the glitter, the fake sculpture, the rain that had started the whole stew, James Roybal, Peter Summers and half a dozen more.

On the hot pink pad she made notes about the safe deposit box theft: Phelps Construction, Phelps himself (now dead), the boxes that were drilled and rifled, the box holders, Marlene Reese, Billy Dawson, Howard Jacobs, the reflections in the marble floor, and again James Roybal and Peter Summers.

And neon blue for the loan fraud: Peter Summers, Congressman Dawson, Frank Freund, now dead, and the girl, Vivian May. Wynn added Mark Bowles to that batch for good measure; he was one of the pieces, after all.

She regarded the colors on her desk, individual squares forming larger blocks, but her fatigue jumbled them. They were too close to her, and to each other. Gathering each block by color, she stuck the chartreuse notes onto the books on the shelves. Hot pinks, the double whammy, she pinned to the cork board in front of her. The bright blues she stuck to the wall above the printer.

For the next half hour she walked from color to color, pink to blue and green and back again, trying to see a connection. Summers' name came up in all of them, so he was the obvious choice. But while he appeared to be part of the loan fraud, he came across as the victim in the double whammy and was mum on the sculpture theft.

Back and forth she went, visiting each side of the triangle over and over, each step bringing more confusion and fatigue, the muddle and tiredness she knew would trigger her dyslexia.

Let it come. It served me well in wine country. And it can't make this case any more of a mess than it already is.

Standing in the middle of the room, she turned in a circle, looking at one color block and then another, until her perception began to shift. In her view, the colors moved and morphed until it seemed they hung in the air around her as though the case and its components were a mobile sculpture in midair in her office; each set of colored notes suspended from an invisible crossbar, each crossbar balancing the others, a careful counterweight that, if taken away, would cause the others to fall.

A theft of a giant fake.

A safe deposit box heist that was meant to be discovered.

And a loan fraud that was sure to be found out.

A balance. That was the connection.

What was it Gio Leo had said? "A side hustle with a big payday around the corner. When that comes in, they'll replace the money or compensate for whatever was stolen."

Was each of these incidents a side hustle for the others? Was the loan fraud a side hustle for the double whammy? Was the sculpture theft...or was there a main game that these were all hustles for?

Wynn shook her head. There had to be something bigger—a better reason for all of this chicanery and smokescreen. Putting her palms over her eyes, she inhaled, and then dropped her hands and shook them.

She turned first clockwise, and then counter-clockwise, under the mobile sculpture in her mind.

Stopping suddenly, she looked up.

Balance.

And the whole thing hangs from the top. Without the top to hook it on, the whole thing falls.

She reached for the phone.

Mark Bowles' wife wasn't pleased when his phone rang in the early hours of the morning. She was even less happy that he had been in such a hurry to grab the phone—ripping off his CPAP mask so that it still hung from one ear when he answered it. But her anger came to a full whistling boil when the caller turned out to be a woman she'd never met—she could hear the voice, even though Bowles held the phone close to his ear—a woman who talked a mile a minute.

Bowles finally turned to his wife and kissed her. "I have to take this. It's about the case." He kissed her again. "I'll go downstairs. Go back to sleep."

He padded downstairs, barefoot, bare-chested, and perched on a kitchen stool at the island. "Okay, Wynn. Wynn, slow down. No, stop. Okay. What's going on?"

"Mark?" Wynn gulped. "Tell me everything you know about Howard Jacobs."

Chapter Thirty-Six

By eight o'clock that morning, the two of them were back in Grazer's office. Grazer once again waggled an empty coffee cup as Wynn and Bowles each presented their separate arguments.

"Summers has his fingers in each of the pies," Bowles said. "You don't have to look any farther."

Wynn shook her head. "He's hardly a criminal mastermind. I've requested a subpoena for his bank account, separate from the audit files. But I'm willing to bet that when we get the account records, we'll see that Summers hasn't made a dime off any of these crimes."

"Then what's your theory, Cabot?" Grazer asked.

Wynn stared directly at her boss. "Howard Jacobs, the bank's president. Or, someone even higher up."

"Based on what?"

Wynn sighed and shrugged. "Gut hunch."

"That's the best you can do? Because...because I need a lot more than your lower GI system telling me I can pull him in. And don't even think about Dawson. I'm still working on that one, and I could have my backside sliced off for it. I'd just as soon work it off in the gym. So come on, talk to me."

Bowles began. "Jacobs opened Nova Bank seven years ago. Of course, the process started even years before that. It takes forever to get through the filing and approval process. Since 9/11, regulators are watching like weasels for terrorists and money-laundering operations."

Grazer chuckled. "Anybody who's applied for a mortgage in the last nineteen years knows that."

Bowles nodded. "Plus, you have to get your Board of Directors together, and prove you have adequate capital."

"Where did the money come from?"

"Family money, near as we can tell," Bowles said.

"Although we're running that down, too," Wynn said. "From what Mark tells me, the Jacobs family came by their money in the eighties and nineties. Mark also says Jacobs is a social climber of the first stripe."

"I always had to get him fifty-yard seats at the Redskins and dugout seats at Nats games. He'd give me a list of Kennedy Center stuff and demand I find out who was going to be there."

"Elbow-rubber," Grazer said.

Wynn smiled. "Yep. Well, when you apply for a bank charter, you have to put down what market you're going to serve. Rumor has it, Jacobs put down the D.C. elite. Not just new rich, he fancied rubbing his funny bone with the old guard."

"Okay," Grazer said, "then if the bank's having problems…"

Wynn nodded. "Bad enough to do loan fraud…"

"Check it out. Be thorough, and be accurate."

"I still think you're wrong," Bowles said. "I still think Summers is your guy."

Grazer stood, signaling the end of the meeting. "But here's the deal. We won't know until you find out. So get out of my office—you can't find out sitting here yapping." She glanced over Wynn's shoulder. Her assistant stood in the doorway, his usual smirk in place. "What is it?"

"Sorry to interrupt, ma'am," he said, though his face said he wasn't sorry at all. "Ms. Cabot has a visitor downstairs."

"James Roybal, reporting as ordered," he said through gritted teeth. The whites of his eyes were red, the lids themselves so swollen it was obvious Roybal could barely see. The parts of his face that weren't bruised were bruised raspberry pink, mottling to yellow and green.

Wynn hustled Roybal into an interview room, where he sat gingerly at the end of a table while she took a chair on one side and Bowles grabbed one across from her.

Roybal nodded to Bowles. "Good to see you."

"You look like hell," Bowles said.

"Well," Roybal grimaced as he shifted his weight, "it's an old line, but you should see the other guy."

Wynn sat forward. "Mr. Roybal, do you need medical attention?"

Roybal took a slow, deep breath. "No, I'm good. I spent the weekend in bed, mostly. He flexed and straightened his fingers. "Trying to get things moving again. Monday and yesterday I called in sick and took it easy. Funny, though, when I called the bank, they told me Marlene took some time off, too. Hey, you don't suppose—"

Wynn turned to the two-way mirror, held a hand up to her cheek, thumb and pinkie splayed in the "call" gesture, pursed her lips and made a note. "We'll check on her." She hoped someone would try to reach Marlene Reese, to verify that she was okay.

"But me," Roybal said, "I'm fine. I'm here, aren't I?"

"You're here because our computer specialists have enhanced the images reflected in the bank floor video on the day of the heist," Wynn explained.

Roybal said nothing.

"Mr. Roybal—"

"James," Roybal said.

"James, I don't have any choice but to name you as part of the theft ring. The bank will probably press charges."

"Even though I got rooked into it?"

"You're an accessory," Bowles said.

Roybal shook his head. "I risked everything—*everything*—to do what some joker calls my patriotic duty, and this is what I get?"

"We need something more," Wynn said.

Bowles toyed with the file folder in front of him. "Give us something, man. Right now it's your word against a Congressman's."

Wynn sighed. "And that probably won't end well for you."

"Ended fine Friday night," Roybal said.

Wynn and Bowles looked at each other and frowned.

"I need some insurance," Roybal said. "I need somebody's word, here, that you'll help me with, with…any charges."

"We're not in a position to make deals right now," Wynn said. "Do you want an attorney?"

Roybal grimaced as he changed position. "No, if the FBI can't help me fight Congress, I'm screwed."

Wynn leaned back in her chair and folded her arms. "How did you get your injuries?"

"If I tell you…"

"All I can promise is that we'll do everything we can."

"It was Sam. Dawson's goon."

"Sam…"

"Don't know his last name. He's, like, Dawson's bodyguard, his driver, his muscle. Friday night I'm at home, late, and he breaks into my apartment." Roybal shrugged. "I jumped him. He's pretty good, but I'm better. I used some moves he never expected."

Bowles smiled. "I don't doubt it—you probably gave better than you got."

"I meant it when I said you should see the other guy. I got him a couple of good body shots."

Wynn and Bowles winced in tandem.

Bowles shook his head. "You're sure it was Sam?"

"I got a good look at him when I chucked his sorry ass into the hallway. It was Sam, all right. And if he's still alive, he's somewhere with a ruptured spleen and pissing blood from kidney damage." Roybal cradled one hand inside the other. "I'm telling you, if he's not in a hospital, he's at the morgue."

Wynn watched Bowles pale, breathing through his mouth as he had at Frank Freund's house.

"James, if we find him, would you be willing to press charges? Because," she laughed at herself, "here's the deal. If you do, we can get his DNA to compare in a couple of other deaths from last week. And that, we can take to Congress."

Roybal exhaled. "Then damn straight I will."

* * *

After her Friday night encounter with Sam, Marlene Reese was not only still alive but enjoying her train ride to FBI headquarters. Her book lay open on her lap, and she looked to others on the train as though she was reading, but in truth she debated how much to tell Agent Cabot about the events of last Friday night.

Her previous interrogation by the FBI had unnerved her, no doubt about it. Still, years of moving through Washington society, with all of its politics, had honed her skills for telling tall tales that were taken as gospel and, in this case, telling close to the truth and being thoroughly disbelieved.

She smiled at that.

After the usual preliminaries of security—Mark Bowles gave Marlene a big hug—Wynn greeted the woman with a smile of relief. "We're glad to see you, Ms. Reese."

"I said I'd be here. I'm glad to help out, however I can."

"So, let me ask first if you've been threatened or attacked in the last week."

"I—I beg your pardon?"

"Mr. Roybal was attacked. Another man was found dead—guy by the name of Phelps. And—" Wynn paused, studying Marlene's reaction. She'd winced at the news of Phelps' murder—did she know the man? "We need to know if you've been attacked."

Marlene looked first at Mark Bowles, and then at Wynn. Her bottom lip trembled.

"Why no, Agent Cabot. I've had nothing like that at all. I've been…safe at home."

* * *

They found Sam, whose unlikely last name was Goodlove, at United Medical Center in Congress Heights. Roybal's diagnosis was spot on, yet not as bad as he'd boasted. There was some damage to Goodlove's spleen and one kidney, but now that several days had passed since the fight, the medics said he could be discharged in the next twenty-four hours if his signs stayed stable.

Since all the FBI had going in was an assault charge, Wynn turned the arrest over to MPD. Frosty Winters pledged two uniforms to do the deed.

"More important, get a cheek swab," Wynn said.

"Will do," Winters said, "but hustle your butt over there before they kick him out."

Wynn arrived as the uniforms were leaving. "Which one of you has the swab?"

The taller of the two held out the vial.

Wynn turned to the other. "Can you stick around and Mirandize him? I want to ask him some questions. And I'll make it good with Winters." She led the officer into the room, listened while he read Goodlove his rights, and confirmed it when Goodlove said he didn't need "no freakin' attorney."

"Mr. Goodlove, you sustained some serious injuries," she said as she dragged a chair to his bed.

"I fell off my bike," Goodlove said.

"That's odd, because there's no damage to your bike. Your injuries aren't consistent with a fall."

He turned his face away from her.

"This fall, did it happen after you left Mr. Roybal's apartment?"

"Don't know what you're talking about."

"Well, see, the problem with that is, the neighbors got a good look at you when…when you left there. And I'm sure, now that we have your DNA, we can prove you've been in Mr. Roybal's unit."

He turned back to her. "You don't know what you're messing with, lady. Sure, I've been in Roybal's place. I was there with a congressman, maybe you've heard of him—Congressman Billy Dawson. You want to know what's going on, you talk to him."

Wynn frowned for dramatic effect. "That's the weird part, Sam. I called the congressman's office and they swear they never heard of you."

"Of course, they'd say that. I work for the congressman himself. He takes care of me."

"Really?" Wynn gestured in an arc around the room. "Who's paying for all this? Because I have to tell you, on my way up here, I stopped at Patient Services and they said you're on your own for this. All the CAT scans and

MRIs, all the X-rays and lab tests, not to mention the hospital stay for what, five days now at a thousand bucks a day—"

"You're lying."

She pointed to her own face. "This is me, not lying. Telling the truth." Leaning forward, she lowered her voice. "He's cut you loose, Sam. He's going to say he knows nothing about you."

Goodlove remembered the scene with Roybal and Dawson outside the Congressional Office Building, and knew too well that Billy Dawson could, and would, do just that. He crumpled. "What's going to happen to me?"

"You'll be discharged from here into the custody of the MPD and held for assaulting James Roybal—at least until we lift your DNA from the bodies of Frank Freund and Narville Phelps. And we'll look to see what we can find on what's left of Rima Arazi."

At the mention of those names, Goodlove's head snapped around.

"Wow, Sam," Wynn said. "You're really pale. I'll get a nurse."

That night, Bishop's phone rang twelve times before it rolled to voice mail.

Wynn waited for the greeting and left her usual breezy plea. "Hey André, it's Wynn. Just checking to see how you're doing. Hope you're on the mend. Give me a call when—well, when you feel up to it."

On his end, Bishop didn't hear the phone ring. His Jerusalem files had arrived via FBI legal attaché and he was engrossed in the file about the case that had taken him to... *Can't think about that right now.*

But something about the file nagged at him at the corners of his mind, something that meant... *Sooner or later, you're going to have to think about it.*

When he finally gave up on the file and looked at the phone, saw the message indicator and listened to her voice mail, he sighed in frustration.

Sooner, then, he said to himself. *I'm almost there.*

Chapter Thirty-Seven

On Thursday, having gone through her notes for the umpteenth time, Wynn took her file and her phone to the cafeteria for lunch. Grazer called. "Stay put," she said. "I'll be there in five minutes."

Grazer marched up to the table with a smirk she usually reserved for her assistant. She clutched a sheet of paper in one hand and pulled out a chair with the other. "I've got good news, bad news and better news."

"Lay it all on me, in that order."

"The first good news is, the lab rats actually do know how to stamp something 'RUSH' when they want to. The bad news is, it takes one of our own guys being killed to get the DNA results this fast."

"And?"

"The second good news is, Goodlove's DNA matches the bruise DNA on Narville Phelps."

"That it?"

"I got the best news of all: Goodlove's a match for bruise DNA on Frank Freund."

* * *

Bishop watched Wynn pace in front of the food truck as he approached. She turned and strode toward him.

"There you are—finally."

"Good morning to you, too."

"Okay, okay," she said, "thank you for coming."

"How could I refuse when you asked so nicely? 'Must see you, come immediately.'"

"Sorry, it's important."

"Then maybe you should talk to Grazer."

"No, I need to talk to you. Look, I know you're having trouble—"

"I'm fine. Getting better every day."

"I know you must be going through some—"

"You have no idea, okay? None. I'm fine. But I'm more than a little on edge."

"My point exactly."

"What?"

"I realize your assignment is above my pay grade. That's no reason for you to shut me out personally."

"Maybe I did. But then you were insubordinate to Grazer? How do you think that made me feel, when I tried to defend you?"

She thought. "All right, maybe I didn't handle this as well as I might have, but now we're both on proba—"

"You shouldn't have tracked me down."

Silence settled like humidity until Wynn spoke. "I apologize. To you. Not to Grazer or the Bureau, but to you. I'm sorry if it made your recuperation harder."

He sighed. "It wasn't all bad, knowing you were there."

"I had good intentions."

"But you weren't doing me, or yourself, any favors. I have to say, I hate being on probation. I want to be back out there, in the field—but I can't until my medical clearance comes through."

Wynn frowned. "And I can only do what's approved, and vetted, and considered. I can't do what I think is right because it gets me in trouble with Grazer. I had a breakthrough last night, but I can't move on it because of politics and bureaucracy."

"Bureaucracy is what bureaucrats do." He grinned at her. "So tell me. What was this breakthrough? Another one of your brain miracles?"

"I need your help, André."

"I don't know if we should—"

"Look," she said. "If I can solve this case, maybe someday I'll have a chance of getting off probation. But without your help, I'm doomed. Just hear me out. Then, if you tell me to go to Grazer, I will, I promise. Only let me bounce this off you first."

He thought for a moment. "I could use your 3-D thinking on my case, too. Let me call Grazer." When she objected, he raised a hand. "I need her permission to read you in. Let me handle it."

Wynn watched him as he walked away, phone to his ear. He leaned against a wall for several minutes and then rang off. "Okay," he said when he joined her again, "we'll trade. You talk first."

As they walked back to the building, Wynn laid out the case for Bishop again, sure that this time she had his attention. As they reached Bishop's desk, she finished with the final broad strokes and pared down her observations.

"No one part of it seems to make any sense on its own," she said. "First, we have the theft that wasn't a theft of a valuable sculpture that wasn't valuable."

Bishop sat and pulled out a tablet. "You have to look at the *why*. Why would someone want to get rid of a fake sculpture?"

"Because they were passing it off as real and didn't want someone to find out."

"Why do you keep someone in the dark about a thing like that?"

"To fool the public or potential thieves? An insurance claim, maybe?" She shook her head. "Then we have a safe deposit box heist that no one will take responsibility for, of items that no one wants to report missing."

Bishop yanked a tissue out of the box on his desk and dabbed at the end of his nose. "But you said everybody involved claims they were under orders from Congressman Dawson."

"Yes, and now we know that two men are dead and at least one other was attacked by Dawson's...uh, persuader, but those aren't ours to prosecute." She ticked points off on her fingers. "Now, it's true, all of this has led to uncovering deeper crimes at the bank: the credit fraud, and unauthorized withdrawals from dormant accounts. But there has to be a connection to all of it and I can't quite place what it is."

"I can tell from that look in your eyes, though. You have a theory."

Leaning on Bishop's desk, Wynn added another finger to her points. "They're all connected, not coincidental. I have to think that one piece may be a side hustle for another one, or the other one may be a side hustle for the first, and they're all balancing each other in this very delicate assemblage. And it all seems to hang from the top—which has to be Nova's president, Howard Jacobs."

"But a lot of it points to Dawson, too."

"And while you say Jake Osborne wants us to go after Dawson with everything we've got, Grazer told me to back off." She sat back. "I have nothing, André. Practically nothing that I can make a case out of, or prosecute." She sighed. "Nothing...with which to redeem myself."

"Sometimes the job gets frustrating. I've told you that."

"This is beyond frustrating."

He nodded. "I'll see if I can find anything—"

She smiled. "Thanks. Now, what can I help *you* with?"

Bishop folded his arms, debating what to tell her. After a moment, he decided that in order to utilize her special way of thinking, he'd opt for more detail rather than a sketchy outline.

"Back in 1995, two religious artifacts were stolen from a synagogue in a place called Nablus, in Palestine. One was a codex from the 15th century, a thick book with a leather cover. We got word a few months back it was in the U.S.—in D.C., actually. That's when I was assigned to the case."

"Without me."

"Wynn, there was an international angle, and I have a little more background—"

"I'm cool. Go on."

"Then we heard about another artifact—an ancient Torah from about 1350. That piece was still in Israel, being offered for sale on the dark web. We watched the web, and an American buyer was found. I joined forces with the Israel Police to be present at the buy..."

"And it...didn't go as planned."

"Precisely, Agent Obvious. Anyway, the buyer took off with the scroll and ended up stateside. Ultimately it moved again—though we're not sure who moved it or how—and the NSA started listening for buzz on international communications. I'm sure that's how Jake Osborne heard about it—and now it's rumored that the Torah is going to be sent back to the Middle East."

"Back to the seller?"

"I don't know. I want to make sure it goes back to its rightful owners, back to the synagogue in Palestine." He spread his hands. "But I can't find it."

"Seamus says international shipments have tons of paperwork—permits and carnets and so forth."

He shook his head. "No way it's going legally. It'll be smuggled. I've talked to my contacts in the black market and dark web—all I can find out is that it's being set up by a woman named Polly."

She frowned. The name rang no bells at all.

"She's either in deep cover or hiding in plain sight, they say. All anybody knows about her is that she's an older woman—not what you'd expect an international play-caller to be— and that she should have a fresh scar on her forehead."

Scar. Why was that part familiar? Her brain started thumbing through the cast of players, putting a scar on each forehead, until—

Wait. There was someone. But it couldn't be, could it? Not pleasant, harmless, grandmotherly—

Marlene Reese.

Wynn's face registered surprise. "There's a woman at the bank, she manages the safe deposit boxes."

"Perfect place to watchdog items coming and going."

"But, but she's—easygoing and soft-spoken. And she said she was taking orders from Dawson."

"The kind you have to watch out for. Let's dig into her and see if she's lying about anything else. Start with international travel. Where's she been lately?"

Summers entered the interview room and took the same chair he'd had before, but unlike his previous visit, no sweat poured down his temples, no perspiration stains darkened his shirt. The whole sordid mess was coming to an end, he thought, at least his part of it anyway, and he would survive.

He didn't want to say anything—wanted to remain closed-mouthed. Denial would mean they couldn't trace anything back to him. But the Suspicious Activity Reports that Bowles had filed pretty much laid everything bare, with Summers' own name at the bottom.

So he would admit to some creative financing—so what? What could happen? At worst, a few weeks or months in one of those federal facilities for white-collar criminals?

Hell, word had it, those places were like country clubs these days: you watched TV, read the Washington Post, worked out regularly. Played bocce ball. They served kosher food. He might make some valuable contacts "inside." And when he got out, he'd have the air, the cachet, the marquee value of having done time.

He looked at the others around the table each in turn—Grazer, Cabot, Bishop and Bowles—and drew in the long, deep inhale he thought a hardened criminal would take.

At least the Cabot woman had displayed the presence of mind to call his attorney and explain the facts. His attorney, now sitting beside him, had urged Summers to consider giving a statement. The FBI agreed Summers could help his own case by giving them something.

Or someone.

Summers cleared his throat. "I am here on the advice of my attorney, and my statement is as follows: I created the credit documents and sent out the money at the bidding of Congressman B. Crawford Dawson. When the money came back into the bank, it was deposited in Congressman Dawson's personal, numbered-only account." He folded his arms.

"Told you," Bowles sang under his breath.

"Here's the deal, Summers," Grazer said. "You had help. We know you did."

Summers started to reply, but his attorney slid his palm sideways across the tabletop, and Summers checked his remark.

"Someone ordered you to do this," Wynn said. "Was it Howard Jacobs?"

Summers scoffed. Only he had been able to resist Jacobs' abuse, the spoiled-child antics he pulled. In all likelihood, Summers believed, he was the only one tough enough to take the fall for this. And surely, he thought, if he kept Jacobs out of this, Jacobs would reward him. So he waved off the question, and silence grew in the room like a bad odor.

Finally, Grazer had enough. "Look, we don't need you to take down Dawson." She rose to exit and pointed her pen at Bowles. "You're with me, right now."

Bowles jumped to the door and when he opened it for her, Wynn followed.

"Not you, Cabot," Grazer said. "What part of 'I will deal with Dawson' do you not get?"

* * *

Linda Grazer went over her notes again: Roybal's story about Dawson coordinating the safe-deposit box heist. Now that they knew Dawson held a numbered account at the bank. The RNC's insistence that the FBI "back off" whatever investigation they had on Dawson. All of it reeked of corruption, but she couldn't prove it, even with the diagram Frank Freund had sent right before he was killed—the diagram that showed money being moved out of Nova, and then back into Dawson's anonymous account at Nova.

She pointed her pen at Bowles, seated across from her. "Your SARs—where did the money come from, again?"

"Inactive accounts, and accounts of folks who weren't in a position to protect their money."

"Right." Grazer wrote while she thought. "Who made the transfers?"

"Ah…let me think. Right, it was a teller named Vivian May. Hasn't been with the bank long—maybe three months."

Grazer wrote. "Still there?"

"To my knowledge."

"Who hired Vivian May?"

"I was in Public Relations, so…" Bowles shrugged.

"So, who did?"

"Summers, I guess. We didn't have a Human Resources person."

"Can you get me the paperwork on Dawson's numbered account?"

"I can't—but someone at FinCEN can."

"Do it. I need to know where that money went when it came back into the U.S."

"I thought we decided it was Dawson's?"

Grazer rolled her eyes. "Look, Bowles, I'll do the deciding. Get me the file. Chop."

She picked up her phone and scrolled through the programmed numbers until she found the one she sought—Linden Schmitz, the man who had resigned as Director of the Office of Government Ethics some years back. Schmitz had been elected to the House two years ago, and sat, of course, on its Ethics Committee. Grazer had her own connections, and sometimes they went deep.

"Schmitz," she snapped when he answered the phone, "tell me something. You ever suspect B. Crawford Dawson of graft?"

Marlene Reese hadn't seen Rima Arazi's brief death notice in the Washington Post. If she had, she wouldn't have known what killed the Palestinian woman or that her body was found outside Nova Bank.

Instead, on Friday morning, Marlene called in sick to the bank, rolled the codex and Torah scroll in the very newspaper that contained Rima Arazi's death notice, wrapped the bulky package in brown paper, trussed it with kitchen twine, and addressed it to Rima Arazi's flat in London.

Her phone rang and she checked the number—Unknown Caller, D.C. number. She dismissed it and then blocked the number—whoever it was had called three times in the past two days.

She phoned an Uber and took her lumpy parcel to the main post office, so that the parcel might go unnoticed in the routine sifting of thousands of other packages bound for world-wide destinations. She filled in the customs paperwork, marked it as a gift and not for resale, paid the breath-taking postage fee, and returned home, looking forward to a peaceful weekend.

She sat down at her computer and wrote an email to Benny Tsedaka, the elderly Samaritan whose life work had been consumed with the search for the Torah scrolls and codex, since their theft in 1995.

"Shabbat shalom," she began. "I hope this finds you well. The Torah and codex are beginning their journey back to Nablus, in the care of Rima Arazi," she wrote, not knowing that the only thing Rima Arazi was on the receiving end of was a stiff neck.

The package made it as far as the central London sorting office by the following Tuesday. And then it disappeared.

Congressman B. Crawford Dawson hit the red "end call" icon. Shaking with anger and frustration, he withdrew a white linen pocket handkerchief from his suit coat and dabbed at his upper lip and brow. There had to be a way out of this. "This" being he didn't know what, but something was coming.

FBI agent Linda Grazer had been adamant—Dawson could come down to FBI headquarters for a chat at her invitation, or he could come under more forceful circumstances. He asked why; she equivocated. He demanded to know the reason for her call; she said she would let him know when he got to her office.

After some bobbing and weaving about scheduling—a floor vote that morning and campaign rallies in Georgia later in the week—they settled on a time. A time that was all too soon to suit Dawson—that afternoon.

Linda Grazer leaned back in her office chair and stared at Dawson for a long moment. She liked that move—it always seemed to make people uneasy. "How many years have you been on the board of Nova Bank?"

"I'd have to check," Dawson said, "but it's been some time. Shortly after they opened their doors."

"And did you have anything to do with either the purchase or the disposition of their sculpture—the *Cornucopia*?"

Dawson chuckled. "I am far from a connoisseur of fine art, Agent Grazer."

He'd dragged out his chewy Southern drawl for the occasion, Grazer noticed, and his shoulders relaxed. Just as she'd suspected—Dawson thought he could charm his way out of this. She made a note. "Did you have anything in the safe-deposit boxes at the bank? The boxes that were recently looted?"

"No."

Grazer wrote again and then looked up at him. "Do you have any bank accounts with Nova? And I warn you here, Congressman, be careful with your answer."

"None in my name."

Grazer smiled and lowered her voice. "That was clever, sir. I'd say too clever. You want to have another run at that answer?"

"No."

Grazer stared at him again. "I understand you're in line for the nomination as vice president at the convention."

"I'm proud to say I am."

"So I'll phrase my question this way—do you hold *any* bank accounts with Nova Bank?"

Dawson shifted in his chair, cradled his chin in his hand and frowned.

Grazer smiled to herself—if this guy thought he was convincing her with this act, he was a very bad actor. She waited.

"No," he said at last, "I can't think of any. Maybe a little petty cash account that my chief of staff might have opened?"

Grazer cocked her head. "Really. I was contacted recently by the Republican National Committee, about our investigation into Nova Bank. I wondered what you might have to say about that—you being on the bank's board, and a Republican."

"I'm aware that there have been irregularities at the bank, of course—the sculpture going missing and the safe-deposit box...uh, situation."

"That's not what I'm asking here, though, is it?"

"I've already answered your question about whether I have...or had...any accounts with the bank. I'd think to do that would be a conflict of interest, wouldn't you?"

"I'd think so, but I'm sure it's happened with other banks and other directors." She shifted gears. "Do you know Peter Summers personally?"

"No. Only in a professional capacity."

"Ah. Never been to any of his parties, or attended sporting events with him?"

"Oh my, no. I can't think we've ever even spoken to each other outside of the board room."

Another smile played at the right corner of Grazer's mouth. "Really. Really?

And how about Howard Jacobs—ever gone to dinner with the Jacobses? Maybe at the Palm?"

"Yes, I do recall once—but that was with a very large group of folks. We were celebrating something. I can't remember now what it was."

Grazer checked her notes. "Congressman, do you accept a salary for sitting on Nova Bank's board of directors?"

"Why do you ask? The—"

"I ask because the House Ethics Rules state very specifically that you may sit on a board, but you may not accept a salary for it. So do you or do you not get paid?"

Dawson reached for his briefcase. "This is very time-consuming, Agent Grazer. I appreciate your thoroughness with your investigation into whatever it is, however I assure you Nova Bank is completely scandal-free. Its board of directors has worked diligently—indeed, tirelessly—to see to it. I need to get back to the Hill, so if you'll excuse—"

"Not quite yet, sir. Here's the deal—I'll ask you one more time whether you have an account at Nova Bank, and whether you get paid for sitting on its board. After I get your answers to those questions, yes or no, I'll tell you why you're here."

Grazer noted the sudden flush in Dawson's face, and his jaw came forward. Good. She'd gotten to him. "Let's take them one at a time. Do you have an account with Nova Bank? In your name or in an anonymous account or in an alias name or in any other way?"

"No."

"Interesting answer, 'no,' because you had a chance to tell the truth just then, and you didn't. Am I right?" Grazer opened a file folder that lay in front of her. On top lay a photograph of Dawson, seated between Howard and Sherryl Jacobs at a table at the Palm restaurant. Clearly no one else was dining with them. She held the photo up for Dawson to see. "When was this taken?" She held up another photo—Peter Summers and Dawson at a Nat's baseball game. "And this?" She folded her fingers across the file. "We have more. Including recent canceled checks for your salary as a board member. You endorsed those checks."

"You have nothing. A couple of photos and some penny ante checks. So what?"

"I have more than a couple of photos, Congressman. And your salary as a board member wasn't what I'd call 'penny ante.' I understand you were being investigated by the House Ethics Committee—until they were pressured to close their investigation. When they saw what I sent, they—"

"That's defamation. You'll never prove it."

"Excuse me—I was talking. The Ethics Committee didn't want to press their findings until they saw what I showed them. They realized that our file, combined with what they already had, proved a conclusive case, and should be made public unless..."

Dawson rolled his eyes and gave an exasperated sighed. "Unless *what*, Agent Grazer?"

Grazer leaned forward, elbows on her desk, hands calmly folded. "The Ethics Committee and the FBI came to an agreement on how it will go for you, if you want to avoid prosecution: You'll withdraw your bid to be on the GOP ticket as Vice President *tomorrow morning* and dismantle your campaign to be reelected to Congress."

Dawson gasped. "I'll do nothing of the—"

"I'm not finished. You'll get a House censure in the brief session between Thanksgiving and Christmas, when no one is paying attention to politics. In January, when the new session of Congress convenes, someone else will be sitting in your chair. You'll go home to Georgia and that will be that for 'Congressman' Dawson. You'll have a nice life as a lobbyist for the cotton farmers for a few years before you retire."

"What a joke. You think you have that kind of power? Let me tell you, lady—" Dawson rose from his chair, jabbing a finger in Grazer's face.

"Sit down, sir, or I'll call for you to be restrained while we talk."

Dawson sat.

"We have proof that you've been taking a salary for sitting on Nova Bank's board and that you hold a numbered account at the bank. We have proof that you have been receiving extraordinary sums of cash in that numbered account transferred from off-shore accounts. That amounts to money laundering. And then similar amounts are transferred out of the numbered account and into the account for your Congressional campaign. That's a violation of campaign finance laws."

"Proof. Bah. What proof do you have?"

"In addition to what we have from our auditors, we have statements from Peter Summers and Vivian May, the teller who made the transfers out of the bank and back into your account. Ms. May also took care of some other details for you, I believe."

"Clerical work."

"If that's what you want to call it. I call it sexual favors. Seems Ms. May took some pictures, too. Pictures of you." Grazer reached into the folder again. "Would you like to see those?"

Dawson swallowed hard. "You say these things have been sent up to the Ethics Committee?"

"They have. Our deal for you to avoid prosecution is on the table, sir. If you don't close up shop, and I mean pronto, the whole mess goes public."

"Polly said she'd set this up seamlessly. That she—"

"Who's Polly?"

"I'm out of the running for Vice?"

"You are. Your Congressional career is over."

"Fuckin' Jake Osborne have anything to do with this?"

Grazer shook her head. "Not at all. I never met the man." She paused. "Congressman? Would you like to make a statement?"

Peter Summers felt transformed, somehow. As though he'd been made to play this part. He rehearsed what he would tell Meredith about how their lives would change, considering first the Gruff Bluff—all a mistake, got the wrong guy, righteous indignation. And then no.

Maybe the Downplay would work better with her—really nothing to worry about, a couple of years and then they'd move and begin a new life. Probably not—no. Meredith would leave him before she'd go for that, and Summers didn't want to deal with alimony in addition to trying to find work after he got out of prison.

Maybe the Tearful Confession, and again, no. Tugging at forelocks simply wasn't in his wheelhouse.

In the end, he decided that in his new bad boy image, he'd go with the Blunt Truth—his inevitable prison sentence. Yes, he thought, that approach might reawaken Meredith's long-forgotten affection.

His phone chimed.

"Summers…" Jacobs' seething anxiety was palpable over the phone line. "Hear you've been chatting with the FBI."

"How'd you know that?"

"Vivian called me—said you were called down there. What did you tell them?"

"Nothing they didn't already know. And, Howard? They already know about the credit stuff with Dawson."

"Damn it, Summers, what did you tell them about *me*?"

"Not a damn thing. I kept you entirely out of it."

"Make sure it stays that way."

"Or what, Howard? You'll fire me? Who the hell do you think you're talking to?"

"Now, listen—"

"No, you listen. I'm already taking the fall for you—"

"Oh, that's *so* noble."

"Look—I expect some gratitude. See if you can find a shred of respect—otherwise I might not be finished talking to the FBI. Here's what you're going to do, Howard—you'll make it up to me for this or I spill everything to them."

Jacobs' side of the conversation went silent for a moment and then he said, "What the hell?"

"I mean it, Howard, and I don't want any nickel and dime shit. Don't kick me to the curb. And no token gestures like you gave Marlene. I mean it."

"All right. Okay."

"I'm warning you, I'm *this close* to rolling over."

Jacobs sputtered. "I wouldn't, I've got to find that—" Once again Howard Jacobs found himself talking to a dead line. Summers had already hung up.

Still, there was something Summers had said that niggled at him…*Marlene*. Of course. Marlene would know what happened to the Torah.

In full tornado mode, Grazer charged toward Wynn Cabot's desk. "Who's Polly?"

"We...we don't know," Wynn said. "She's a person of interest in Agent Bishop's—"

Grazer spun toward Bishop's desk. "Bishop—over here."

"Here's the deal," Grazer said, as Bishop crossed to Wynn's desk. "Congressman Dawson told me he's been taking orders from some woman, code named Polly."

"Ah. Polly," Bishop said. "She's supposedly the mastermind moving stolen art back to the Middle East."

"Yeah, well, seems she also works for Nova Bank."

Wynn shot to her feet. "André—Polly *is* Marlene Reese!"

Grazer glowered at the two of them. "Mark Bowles is on his way in. We need to pick her up and chat further. What do we know about her?"

Wynn opened the file to Marlene's data sheet. "She's 64, born in Chicago, came to D.C. twenty years ago. But...this is interesting. She's mentioned in a whole bunch of newspaper articles—look at these, society column stuff. When she hit the D.C. circuit she was quite the doyenne—and always seems to be with another woman. Sandra Cohen. Sandra *Jacobs* Cohen."

Mark Bowles' voice cut in. "Sandy Cohen's maiden name was Jacobs."

"So what's the deal? Were they a couple?"

"It was before my time," Bowles said. "When Jacobs started Nova Bank and hired me, well...I heard the rumors, but...I thought Marlene and Sandy were good friends who shared some political views."

Grazer leaned against Wynn's desk and thought a moment. "Where's Sandra Cohen now?"

"Died, years ago," Bowles said.

Bishop leaned in. "Get a date of death and address at the time, and compare it to where Marlene Reese lived. I'm thinking Polly is a well-connected little lady with a big story to tell."

Grazer straightened. "Get her in here and let's find out."

Wynn and Bishop heard muffled voices as they approached Marlene's apartment in the building on 13th Street NW.

Wynn unsnapped the strap on her shoulder holster. "Sounds like Polly has company," she said. She raised a hand to knock on the door, but it swung open as she touched it. Nodding at Bishop, she pushed the door the rest of the way open. "Ms. Reese? FBI," she called.

Two people stood in the living room: Marlene, on the far side, raised her head to look over the shoulder of the man between her and the door. "Ah, Agent Cabot. How nice to see you. Agent Bishop—you look a good deal healthier than the last time I saw you. Do the two of you know my brother-in-law, Howard Jacobs?"

Jacobs turned to Wynn and Bishop.

His right hand held a gun.

Wynn didn't take her eyes off Jacobs, but off to her right she heard Bishop's gasp, followed by shallow, rapid breathing. She held her arms high, spreading her fingers. "Mr. Jacobs."

"I'm not her brother-in-law," Jacobs growled. "Never that. They couldn't get married back then."

Wynn forced a smile. "It looks like you two were in the middle of something. If this is an awkward time, we'll come back." But she didn't move.

"No, stay," Jacobs said. "We're about to find out what she did with the property she stole from me."

Bishop finally spoke. "Property you stole in a Jerusalem café. Which was already stolen from its home in Palestine."

Jacobs turned the gun on Bishop. "I tried to buy it in a clean deal—paid them what they were asking with no negotiating. But that night they decided they wanted more. When I got the chance, I took it for the original asking price."

Wynn stepped closer to him. "Put the gun down, Mr. Jacobs."

"No. She's got to tell me where she's stashed the Torah."

Marlene tilted her head. "I don't have it, Howard. It's on its way back to Nablus."

"You're lying, Marlene. It can't be—"

Marlene gave a sad chuckle. "Of course it can, you sanctimonious shit. I was the only one who loved Sandy and when she died, all you gave me was a crappy job in a basement."

Jacobs stared at Marlene, his mouth agape. "I have to get the Torah back—I have to get it back, or I'm dead."

Marlene shrugged. "Then you're dead, Howard. I shipped the Torah and the codex out this morning."

"Put the gun down, Jacobs," Wynn said. She closed the gap between them and pivoted on her left foot. Her right hand came up under the gun as her left hand grabbed the barrel and forced it away. With a quick step back, she wrenched the gun from him, took the grip in both hands, and trained it on Jacobs.

She brushed an auburn curl out of her face and smiled at Bishop. "Wow," she said. "That actually worked."

Chapter Thirty-Eight

When Linda Grazer and her arresting officers showed up at Nova Bank that afternoon, flashed credentials at James Roybal, and fanned out over the bank, they began their recitations of Miranda Warnings in the executive offices: "Peter Summers, you are under arrest for money laundering," Grazer began.

Summers wrenched his arm from Grazer's grasp. "I said I'd come peacefully—this is an outrage."

"The FBI is outraged too, Mr. Summers, and our outrage is slightly more legal than yours. Let's go." Over her shoulder she said to one of the agents, "Pick up Vivian May on your way out. If she's hiding in the ladies' room, get Summers' secretary to pry her loose."

"Yes, ma'am," he said. "What about the security guard?"

"He's clean, gave us what we needed."

Peter Summers paled. "James did? James…"

"Yes, Mr. Summers. James Roybal. Very useful. Well, useful to us. Not so much to you or Howard Jacobs, or his…uh…employee, we'll call her—Ms. May."

Summers swallowed hard. "Jacobs is…"

"Being arrested as we speak, sir. On the same charges. Only he's got a bigger problem—he's got a district charge of grand theft, too, so MPD is at the Jacobs residence. I imagine it's quite a show for the neighbors."

"Grand theft for what? You people are out of your league."

"Here's the deal, Summers," Grazer said as she began to walk him toward the front door.

Summers balked. "Can we use the back exit?"

"Excuse me, I was talking," Grazer continued toward the front door. "Here's the deal—we know what happened to the sculpture, and who put the phony one in its place. We know who broke into the safe deposit boxes too, and it's not looking good for you, or Howard Jacobs or Marlene Reese. You and Ms. Reese and Ms. May and Mr. Jacobs will have some time to catch up when you're all together for arraignment on our charges. After you're tried, the District can take their turn."

"B-b-but Vivian..."

"Yes, poor Vivian, caught in the web, eh? No, I'm afraid she was very much in on it. She suggested to Howard Jacobs which accounts were most vulnerable or were dormant. She moved the money, didn't she?"

Summers nodded. "I never questioned how Jacobs knew which accounts we should use."

"Probably pillow talk—Vivian May was a busy girl. Bank accounts weren't the only things being used, were they, Mr. Summers?"

"And Marlene?"

"Is on her way to the Detention Center too, I'm afraid. Marlene was responsible for the safe deposit thefts. She's also, it turns out, quite handy at moving antiquities. Many of the pieces she stole or sold were from the boxes she guarded daily."

Summers gasped. "She was..."

Grazer nodded. "...in Jerusalem on a night when everything went so very wrong. There was quite a bit of shooting that night—in fact, one of my agents was very nearly killed. He placed her at the scene."

"That's how she got the..."

"Yes. The cut on her forehead."

"And then she..."

"Yep—came back to work, had someone break into Jacobs' safe deposit box and steal the Torah and the scroll and then she sent them to...well, she thought she was sending them to Rima Arazi. In fact, they never made it as far as Rima's doorstep—they've disappeared. Again."

Summers' shoulders slumped. "All for Dawson?"

"Some of it, yes. Some of it for Jacobs—he was skimming from Dawson's campaign donations. People died, Summers, and five of you are going to jail. You're damned lucky you didn't get killed yourself. Dawson had a goon named Goodlove who was running around breaking people's necks. He killed Rima Arazi, and our auditor, and the guy who fixed your roof, and he nearly killed James Roybal. MPD has him in a holding cell at the precinct. It isn't as comfy as the digs you'll get, but it gets the job done."

"That's how Roybal ended up with the bruises he had when he came back to work on Wednesday?"

"Roybal got the better end of the deal—put Goodlove in the hospital."

"Figures. Why are you telling me all of this now? Maybe I'll make up some wild story and use these details..."

Grazer chuckled. "No, you won't. You're not that smart. All of this will come out at your trial, with substantiated proof. All this and more. See, we really do have a paper trail that incriminates you, and Jacobs, and Ms. May, and Congressman Dawson."

"Dawson—he's the one who put us up to this. He should..."

"Dawson has cut a deal. You'll never hear his name again."

"So the one who was pulling the strings..."

"Was your boss. Howard Jacobs."

Chapter Thirty-Nine

At an emergency meeting of the Board of Directors of Nova Bank on Saturday morning, July 18, the first item of business was to censure Howard Jacobs and Peter Summers for their criminal activities. Though they had not yet been convicted, the evidence, to the board's satisfaction, was incontrovertible; full cooperation with the authorities was pledged. Although James Roybal was involved, the board decided no mention of his name was necessary. Roybal had, after all, been instrumental in bringing the whole plot down.

The chairman read a letter of resignation from the board written by B. Crawford Dawson, former Congressman. A replacement for Dawson's board seat was nominated and approved unanimously—now that he was no longer on the Senate Finance Committee, and until he was elected Vice President, they would be honored to have Senator Jake Osborne on their board of directors, should he agree to serve.

Finally, one of the old guard asked to speak. "I want the damned sculpture back," she said. "The real one."

Wynn clambered out of the Slow Pocus and fell into step beside Mark Bowles. They moved up the circular driveway of B. Crawford Dawson's Georgian mansion, past the carefully carved topiaries that had no doubt been nippered to perfection by Planties and Bloomers, and up the steps.

She strode into the cavernous entryway, her eyes drawn upward by a staircase, then further up to the ceiling overhead. Her audible gasp made Bowles turn and look at her, then crane his own head to see where she was looking.

And there it was.

The genuine *Cornucopia,* hung in B. Crawford Dawson's entry-way for all to see. Its platinum arms gleamed in artful spotlights; the hanging elements moved in slow, graceful arcs, displaying first one side, then the other. Gold and silver, shining like the emblems of wealth, power and stability they were crafted to be. Lowell Chrysler was a genius, she thought. She dropped her eyes to Bowles. "Wow. I had no idea."

"It was all worth it, I guess. We found the bad guys, even if we couldn't put them all behind bars."

"Yeah. What a mess," she said.

"Thanks for…well, letting me work with you."

Wynn's head turned toward a back-up claxon noise in the brick-paved driveway. "The art transport's here. The real one."

"I feel bad about the way some of this turned out," Bowles said. "About the mess I created and people getting killed and…and about Marlene."

"Don't worry about Marlene, Mark—she's not who you think she is. Never was. And she's not going to prison, but we let Summers and Jacobs and Ms. May think so."

"What…?"

Wynn smiled. "None of us knew, except top brass at headquarters. Marlene Reese was, until last week when we blew her cover, an FBI informant." She withdrew an envelope from her handbag and handed it to Bowles. "Here. The missing photos and emails from your file, I think. Sam Goodlove had them—seems you were next on the list for one of Sam's special massages."

Bowles blew out a sigh of relief. "Thank you, but they're kind of useless now, aren't they?"

"Unless we need them for evidence."

"And the missing SARs?"

"Dunno, but I have my suspicions. Is there any way Jake Osborne had access to those?"

"Not mine, not that I can think of. But certainly he could have access to the duplicates at FinCEN."

"That's my guess, and it's only that—a guess. And because it is, it's just between you and me, okay?"

As they left the Side Hustle, Gio Leo held the door for Wynn.

"I still don't believe I didn't see it," she said. "I couldn't make the connections. Couldn't believe Marlene Reese was—"

"Stop beating yourself up. You caught the bad guys."

"Usually, I can *see* what the angles are, how the parts jibe, but this time, I—"

"Wynn."

"I totally blew it."

"Stop and listen to me." He waited until her eyes focused and met his. "Solving stuff like this is almost always a team effort. You can't take all the blame, any more than you can take all the credit."

"But I—"

"You're too wrapped up in this. I don't know why, but you're so fixated, so obsessed with it, I can't even talk to you."

"I am not fixated." They crossed Seventh St. NW to her car. "Okay, I am, but my boss has a chip on her shoulder, and I've got to close cases or I'm toast."

"You're not—"

"I don't have a side hustle, Gio. This job's all I've got."

"Are you listening to yourself?"

She hugged her handbag to her chest. "You're right. I'm sorry, Gio. I...I need to go home. I'll see you next time."

"Not next time, Wynn." When he saw puzzlement cloud her face, he added, "I can't keep doing this."

"Gio, I might have been—"

"I spend a couple hours with you every now and then, and you aren't even there." He watched a car go by. "I need to know where this is going."

"Wait, what? Why does it have to go anywhere? Why can't we just be—"

"I can't do that. I'm in deeper than friendship. And I'm not a friends-with-benefits kind of guy."

He took a deep breath and placed his hands on her shoulders. "My work-related reasons for being here are wrapped up, and I can't..."

"I'm sorry, I didn't even ask—"

"Yeah, well, I'm going home to California for a while. I think we both need some time apart. You decide you want to come out and see me, you're always welcome." He kissed her on her forehead, tapped her nose with an index finger, turned, and walked away.

Wynn got into her car and sat behind the wheel for a long time. What was it Grazer had said? "The book on you, Cabot, is that you don't think." She needed to think now. She needed balance, and she needed to figure out how to get it.

For that, she'd need time, and clarity.

Time off.

And a swimming pool.

Chapter Forty

She needed to get rid of the tension between her shoulders—a few laps before dinner.

She raised her head from the water as she began to turn for yet another lap and glimpsed a pair of brown oxfords at the pool's edge. She paused and looked up.

Bishop gave her a two-fingered salute, a towel over his shoulder. He knelt. "Hi. Got a sec? I think we need a sit-down."

She pushed wet hair out of her face. "A sit-down?"

"As in, I don't want to say this over the side of a swimming pool, okay?

Wynn pushed herself out of the pool. "What's up?"

Bishop handed her the towel. "In a minute. Let's find someplace...drier."

Once they'd settled in an alcove off the changing rooms, Bishop waited for a group of elderly women carrying pool noodles to pass before he spoke. "I've decided to leave the Bureau."

The news sent a shockwave through her. She gasped and then gaped at him, unable to sort her thoughts. "But, Santa Fe, André. And then Napa, and then this case—we..."

"I know. I knew you wouldn't understand if I just told you on the fly. That's why I want us to talk about it."

"*Us*," she thought. He'd said, "*Us*." She nodded. "Yes, we should talk about it. Give me five while I get dressed. I think I need a glass of wine."

Bishop smiled. "I know just the place—not far from here—a joint called the Side Hustle."

Once again Wynn's eyes widened, and her mind raced. Had he seen her there with Gio Leo? Or was it coincidence? How did he... "I know the place," she said.

"Meet me there in fifteen minutes?"

A Note From the Authors

The Torah scrolls and codex stolen from the Palestinian city of Nablus remain missing today and are widely thought to have been taken apart and sold piecemeal. If you have any information regarding a part of the stolen scroll, or a page or pages thought to be from a Torah scroll, please contact the FBI's Art Crimes Unit, (202) 324-3000, or Interpol, through their website https://www.interpol.int/en/Contacts/Contact-INTERPOL.

There are an estimated 25 million safe deposit boxes in America. No federal laws govern the boxes; no rules require banks to compensate customers if their property is stolen or destroyed.

The authors understand that the events that take place in this book are not as they would have been in the summer of 2020, due to restrictions placed on businesses and the movements of people by COVID-19. In the interest of creating a timeless story we wish to acknowledge the differences but hope the story itself will outlive the limits of coronavirus.

About the Author

Drew Golden is the sister writing duo of Cynthia Drew and Joan Golden. Asheville, North Carolina resident Cynthia Drew is recipient of the 2017 INDIE Gold Award for Best Mystery and is a certified private investigator. Joan Golden is an Albuquerque, New Mexico resident and award-winning screenwriter.

You can connect with me on:

🌐 https://www.levelbestbooks.us/drew-golden.html

Also by Drew Golden

Nouveau Noir

Domaine Laurent's Gamay Nouveau is here and it's killer.Celia Bouchet is hot smoke in silk pajamas, the beautiful daughter of Napa Valley scion Florian Bouchet, owner of Domaine Laurent winery. When two costly paintings in Domaine Laurent's tasting room vanish and then Bouchet himself dies suddenly, his mistress, Napa's most exclusive high-end realtor, and Celia's possessive fiancé can't wait to get their hands on Bouchet's insurance settlement. But by the Friday after Thanksgiving, eight more people across the nation are dead—each of them poisoned after a few sips of Domaine Laurent's celebrated debut vintage Gamay Nouveau. Were the poisonings bio-terrorism? Revenge? Industrial espionage? The FBI moves rookie agent Wynn Cabot into the investigation and she's joined in the hunt by her boss, Special Agent André Bishop. Wynn, whose dyslexia is an asset in puzzle-solving, must solve the case before she herself is murdered or her first case will be her last. Set in the lush wine country of northern California, Nouveau Noir exposes the fascinating detail and vulnerabilities of the wine industry.

CPSIA information can be obtained
at www.ICGtesting.com
Printed in the USA
LVHW031113311220
675393LV00005B/670